Grindley

Richard Buck

First Published in Great Britain in 2013 by Lulu Publishers

This edition published in 2014

This is a second edition

ISBN: 1499146744
ISBN-13: 978-1499146745

"If a book is going to be bad, then it best be short.

If I could write better then I would."

ACKNOWLEDGMENTS

I would dedicate this to the people in my life, but I don't think anyone wanted to be associated to this dribble. If you've made it this far: you're doing well – Cheers

This is intended as a work of fiction

1

I woke in my tiny Leeds apartment and turned onto my side to face Louise - she was still asleep. Carefully, I made my way out of the bed; perching on the side, I gathered my head: fuzzy from the night before. I stood up and made my way to the bathroom.

I splashed some water on my face; threw my dressing gown over my shoulders and made my way into the lounge. The area was still 'busy', along with the hangover from last night: half empty beer bottles littered the side tables and the floor around the sofas. I just walked past it, hardly giving it a look. The smell of warm alcohol was not what I needed first thing in the morning!

On the fridge door was a countdown calendar made up from small sheets of paper. It had on it the date and underneath it displayed how many days until the London Olympics. I tore off the top sheet and read: 238

days till opening ceremony. I opened the fridge: leftovers of a Chinese takeout. I placed the food onto a plate and put it in the microwave. I poured an orange juice and took a sip. It wasn't going to be enough. In the cupboard under the sink was where I kept the spirits. I pulled out the vodka and added it to the orange juice. The microwave pinged at me. I stopped; put down my drink; walked over and opened the microwave. The smell of the reheated food made me gag. I left it in and closed the door. Instead, I sipped at my vodka and orange.

I made my way back into the living room and sat on the sofa. It was winter and cold. I'd lived in nine different houses in the last five years and I'd always been cold when winter came around. I took another sip of my drink and then another. I went to the kitchen and topped up the glass, and then returned to the living area and placed myself carefully down on the sofa.

I looked at my watch: 07.34. I was always up early - always tired - I used to love to sleep in. I'd often stay up late, watching the TV and drinking. Early mornings and little sleep were no cure for hangovers. I was 25 and I looked 35. At the rate I was going, I was never going to make it to 50. I honestly believed that I was halfway through my life. Death didn't frighten me: not as much as the thought of another 25 years.

I could hear Louise moving about; her alarm must have gone off. She would snooze it and grab another ten minutes in bed, but she was always rushing to make it to work. I would look at her every day with envious contempt. Everything seemed so simple and easy for her: get up, go to work, come home. No matter what she did, she could just live in *the* moment and never plan a single thing.

When she came into the room, fussing about as she did, everything was so blissful to her but so slow, and with an annoyingly painful attention to detail. As she went to the kitchen, I knew that she'd say something. I took another sip and waited for it.

"You've left reheated leftovers in the microwave for me?"

"Yes. You can eat them. I know how you always complain you're short on time." That wasn't the reason at all, but if any good could come from the hangover, then I'd take it.

"Well, I don't want leftovers for breakfast, do I?" She asked the question, yet both of us knew that there was no need for reply. I began to get irritated. Little sleep and the hangover from hell were only fuel for bad tempers.

"I was only trying to do something nice for you." This was another lie. But it was easier then getting into a fight. Even if she called my bluff, the argument would have been no worse than the original - so I had nothing to lose.

Louise looked at me. I knew there was something she wanted to say. She held it to herself. I went into the bedroom; found some of my tracksuit bottoms from the day before and a sports top. You could tell that it had been worn. I held them up and smelt the pits and the crotch - it wasn't too bad. I put the clothes on and sprayed deodorant under my arms. From there, I went back into the bathroom; took a mouthful of mouthwash. I picked up my keys from the sideboard in the hall and walked down the stairs to the front door. Outside, I jumped into my Astra.

2

The traffic was shit. I always hated it. A simple six-mile drive took me thirty to forty minutes some mornings. This was one of those mornings. I pulled into a fast food restaurant on my way and the girl who served me looked miserable. She had probably been there since opening time at 5am – still, she looked pretty good for it. Unlike those fat girls who usually work in those places, she had tanned skin and long, dark hair tied back in a ponytail. Her nose was small on her face and dotted with freckles. I couldn't make much of her figure out from under her baggy top and the ordering window sheltered her hips.

I took my time and looked at the menu. The girl seemed impatient with me, as if every moment I took was eating into her precious life. I ordered a large, black coffee with one sugar and a bacon bagel. My stomach had begun to ease as it had had time to settle. I re-joined the traffic and bit into my breakfast.

3

I pulled up to the security guard at the entrance to the athletics track. They were always funny about letting me in. I was supposed to have bought an annual pass for £30. But if I went to the gate each morning, they would always give me a day pass for free.

I wound down my window and looked at the elderly, balding man. Without any words, he gave me a daily pass and an unnecessary gaze of contempt.

There were a few different security guards you could get, depending on what day or time you would pull up to the window. The older ones were usually sterner, making it known to you that they didn't approve of what you were doing. Ripping them off of £30 a year, it wasn't like it was their fucking money. The younger ones didn't care, sometimes they wouldn't even give a damn about you; they would just open the gate and let you in. My favourite was this young lass, she was a little rough round the edges but still do-able. She was the nicest by far and would try to help me out by offering me week-long passes at a time. I could never tell whether it was flirting or not. I would often say very little and just stare at her - I'm sure she liked it and knew exactly what I was thinking. I wish it were her on the gate everyday, purely for the ease of it.

4

The track was always busy in the mornings. Thankfully, my hangover had started to ease. I took a couple of pills to help sort the headache and walked out over to where my training group were.

Compared to some of the groups that worked out down at the track, ours was pretty small. Our coach was a small guy. He always wore a cap and didn't say too much until he had to. He'd been slowly putting on weight since I'd known him, hell, probably even before that. His clothes were old besides the t-shirt he'd been given by his employers. He would sometimes shave once a week but would mainly sport a messy, stubble look.

I placed my small kit bag down on the floor and took out a drinks bottle. It was filled with water. I sat and gulped half of it down. It was the best way to keep breakfast down in case we had too much running to do: get the fluids in early.

I gave a nod of my head to Coach, the kind that two quiet men do to acknowledge one another and then went to do a warm up lap of the track, nothing much, just some slow jogging. I could see the rest of the group already getting into their spikes for the main running session. Like me, they were all sprinters and we all ran the quarter mile event.

They would always be there early. Each of them had

moved closer to the track so they could make training on time. Never mind about the rest of their lives; in fact, I wasn't even too sure if there was anything else to their lives really. They ate, slept and fucked track and field. I could get on-side with fucking track and field. The girls were everywhere: all trim and always wearing tight fitting Lycra. Depending on what sort of chick you wanted, you just picked your event. The sprinters had big bums and flat chests; they were usually tiny and crazy. I imagined them being all sorts of mental in the sack. Endurance girls were just very slim. If you wanted a curvy woman then the throwers had those big curves you could sink your teeth into. They looked like big girls compared to those at that track, but I had seen a few of them on nights out. They held their own against the sedentary population.

There was always the exception to the rule. If a girl was going through a break up, stress from work or university - home problems of almost any kind – then these girls would stop working out for a while. They would usually drink and eat more and put on some weight. It looked pretty good on them; their tits would sprout out and clearly appear through their tight tops, and their arses would grow. Most impressively, they would still fit into tiny Lycra when they came back, even though it was now far too small for them. It would often show a tight outline of everything they had to offer.

By now, my group were well on with the session. I skipped the rest of my warm up and went straight into spikes. The session that day was 100m, 200m, 300m, 400m, 500m, and back down again. I joined the group on the 300m rep going up. I ran it and won the mini race. We took eight minutes and then went to run the 400m; I won that one too. I threw up, then joined the guys for the 500m and then threw up mid-way. I went to the toilets and splashed cold water on my face. By the time I came back out to the track, I'd missed the 400m. I joined in again for the 300m but, this time, just ran off the front-runner. As we came off the final turn into the home straight, I thought about pulling past him. But I decided not to. The fact that I knew I could beat him was enough for me.

We took a further eight minutes and then I forced them to wait another two minutes, as I took my time to get ready to run the 200m. We all ran that one slowly. The final 100m was a flat out race for them; I ran alongside them - everyone was tired and I was hung-over. I did enough so that I didn't fall behind, but gave it no more effort.

Coach came over afterwards and gave a nod of his head. "Good everyone."

"What time was it?"

"How fast was it?"

"What pace was I on for?"

All these questions shot out from the others.

"It was good for this time of year."

I knew what that meant. If we were running it any other time of the year, it would be shit. It's expected though: running high volume, hangovers; fucking minus temperatures.

Coach told us to head into the gym and gave us a weights' program. I took mine and told everyone I'd meet them in there. I drank what was left from my water bottle, still breathing heavily. I walked over to the high jump mats on the back wall of the internal building. It was the darkest place in the centre at that time of day. I laid on one of the mats, closed my eyes and went to sleep.

I woke up an hour or so later to a mostly deserted training centre. 'These fuckers were lazy,' I thought to myself. I made my way over to the gym and looked inside. There were two athletes: both local, lower level. The guy looked like he was maybe eighteen; I thought instantly that they must have been university students trying their hand at workouts between lectures. The girl looked around eighteen/nineteen, she had clearly put on her 'fresher's fifteen'; her arse was squeezed tightly into a pair of Lycra shorts. She was very pale, with red hair and wide hips. The two of them were on the squat rack. He would stand behind her and watch closely each time she squatted. Whenever it was his turn, he'd pile on the weight and try to make it look as easy as possible. She would just look at her phone or pick up a drinks bottle and sit waiting. The dumb shit was obviously interested in her and she didn't give a fuck.

I went on with my program: a bit of bench press. Coach had put down to do a 5, 4, 3, 2 series - getting heavier each time. I decided on doing four, one rep efforts. I put 90kg on the bar and bounced it off my chest. Easy I thought. Then I sat up and watched as Red took to the rack again.

As she went down under the strain of the weight, her knickers became visible through the Lycra; as it stretched and lost its opaque nature. Huge, animal print knickers were showing through.

I put 100kg on the bar this time and again bounced it off my chest, this time taking it down a bit too fast and impacting hard on me. I exhaled sharply as I threw the bar back up. That was enough bench press for me.

I sat there a little longer with the weight still on the bar. I was watching Red and her gimpish admirer do their stuff. Her hips were so wide, I didn't know if her pussy would have enough on it to feel a cock penetrate her. She might have been one of these uni-girls who liked experimenting. She looked dirty to me. Like pure filth. I decided that the gimpish admirer was going to get nowhere. I thought about saying hello. I thought about fucking her, but I didn't do anything about it. I lost interest in the two of them. I lost interest in what I was doing. I decided to get ready for work early. I left the gym and went into the changing rooms.

5

As I set off from training, I was in two minds; I had just over an hour and a half until my shift started at the supermarket: should I take myself home or find somewhere to sit?

As I was driving my regular route, a diversion blocked me off. I followed the diversion part way and then, rather then take the route home, I turned and drove into the city. I slowly came through the busy streets until I saw a 'Free Parking' sign outside a pub. I pulled up, round the back and took myself straight into the bar.

I hadn't been there before. It was quite dark, and relatively empty. A few TVs were bracketed to walls; they were showing music videos from the eighties but with no sound - it was just a silent music video.

"Half a lager," I instructed the barman. He nodded then pulled the drink from the tap.

"That's £1.85, please."

I gave him the two-pound coin I had in my wallet and then took the change. I had a ten pound note still in there, along with a few bits of copper.

I sat in that bar and drank. I went into a time-passing gaze, watching the silent music videos on the screen.

The performers were extending their hands using finger points. I thought to myself 'These guys look like they can really sing'.

On what looked like a ballad of some description, the singer strung together a combination of a fist clench, followed up by a series of finger points at the camera. On what I assumed was the chorus, he instead took his clenched fist and turned it into an open hand that swept in front of him. He did this twice; on the final time, he added a step forward with an open hand swing.

I ordered another half pint and this time I managed to eliminate all conversation on my side of the process. I pointed to my glass.

"Same again?"

I replied with a nod. When the barman brought my drink over, the ten pound note was sitting on the bar. He took it and returned the change.

I left the coins out in front of me but put the five pound note back in my wallet. I returned to drinking. Having my fill of silent music, I turned to think about my life. I revisited ex-girlfriends in my head. I played over situations that were so close - that I could have done differently. I sat thinking up little quotes - some of which I'd probably half-remembered from hearing before. I debated my regrets in life. Are you a better man for having regrets? For knowing you could have done something differently? Or is it best to live life with no regrets and accept that every decision you made was right and shoot through life that way?

I finished off my drink. This time, when I signalled at my empty glass, the barman knew exactly what to do. We eliminated all verbal communication; he gave me my drink; took the money and brought back the change.

I supped at my drink. Nothing much was going through my head. I thought how much I despised the weather, but that was just because it was particularly cold and I couldn't afford to run the heating.

I just sat and thought. I sat and watched. I watched people walking outside, through the small windows. I watched the other drunks sitting in the bar with me. I knocked back the remainder of my drink in a quick series of successive gulps. I then picked up what little change I had left and put it in my back pocket and headed off to work.

6

I parked up in the supermarket car park. I always parked close to the door. I wasn't supposed to but nobody really said anything about it. I was only a temp anyhow and it didn't really matter. I walked in through the main entrance with the rest of the customers. I stopped off at the security desk and chatted to Mike for a while.

Mike was a boxer; he was a pretty big guy, probably

around the same height as me: around six feet two inches. He definitely had a good stone on me though. He had big fists that would make my hands feel small every time we came to shake hands. His hands though were smooth. I thought that being a fighter, he would have battered hands from the gym. My hands were always rough and blistered.

I never talked too much about anything real with Mike; always just asking about his next fight and he'd ask me how the track was going. I'd always tried to avoid talking about it much. I tried not to let anyone know that I did sport. I didn't want to open myself up to conversation from everyone. And those that don't like sport seemed to take a strong dislike to you: if you are a self-confessed sportsman. Plus, I didn't know how many more there were like Mike: people who take it so seriously and it becomes their life. I did feel like it was a good idea to have Mike on side though - he seemed like a pleasant enough guy and who wants to be on the wrong side of a fighter?

We had swipe cards to clock in and out. We had to swipe three minutes before the start of our shift or be docked an hour's pay. I would walk the long way round to my locker so that I could swipe in on my way upstairs. I had to be careful to check that there were no managers following me or that I wasn't spotted by one of the brown-nosing minimum wagers.

I keyed in at two minutes to the hour. I had lost an

entire hour's pay for being less than a minute late.

"Fuck!" Every subsequent fifteen minutes late that I was, I'd lose another hour of pay.

I walked up to my locker and took off my jacket. I found that if I walked into the store without a jacket over my uniform, someone would stop me at least once. I put my car keys, my phone, my wallet and my jacket into a locker. I made a note of which locker I put my gear in. Sometimes I would be so tired or drunk when using the lockers, I would come back and forget which one I'd got my stuff in.

I walked to the department's back stock. There was usually a message from the manager with instructions for the shift. I read down to my name: Grindley: 14.00-00.00. Work short life. Delivery. Fill milk.

I opened up the dairy chiller. There were three sets of seven cages in short life, all in rows lining the perimeter of the chiller. In the centre of the room were a further twenty-five cages of the morning delivery. The manager expected me to work all twenty-one cages of short life so that I could then move the morning delivery onto the outside and put the ten o'clock delivery into the space created in the centre.

Working a cage could take up to an hour, depending how full it was and what it contained. Those cages were heavy. Dragging them out would take a good five minutes each way. The worst thing about dragging the cages out was that the chiller was built down into the ground. So, over the first ten or so metres you had to pull the heavy, full cages uphill.

I picked a cage full of cooked meats first. Cooked meats were fiddly and took a long while to get out. It was a light cage though and easy to pull up the incline. I dragged it to the top of the isle and there were cage locations just set off from the end fixture. Where the clear plastic would come to meet the start of the next refrigerators, I slotted the cage in, opened the door and began to work the cage. I always started from the top - anything that wouldn't go out was classed as 'overs' and I left that on top so I could keep track of what I'd tried to work. The cage took me a solid three quarters of an hour to get through. I dragged it back and began the cycle again, this time with a pizza cage.

I worked straight through till six in the evening. I took my break. We were allowed fifteen minutes for every five hours we worked. You could take them as either two fifteen minute breaks or a half hour break. I took the full thirty minutes; I went upstairs to our cafeteria. It wasn't much. A few tables bundled together next to a makeshift kitchen in a tiny room with no windows.

The food was cheap. It was supposed to be sold to us at cost. I knew they'd still be making something off it. Four biscuits cost twenty-two pence but so did a chip butty. I bought eggs, chips and beans: seventy pence. I walked over to a table near the coffee machine. Put down my food. Then I bought a coffee for twenty-two pence. Nothing was less then twenty-two pence. It was obviously a minimum price they would drop to.

I sat down; picked up a copy of The Sun newspaper and opened it up to page 3: Justine, 24, from Manchester. She was tanned with dark brown hair. There were no tan lines across her breasts. She had obviously taken care to avoid them. She had brown eyes and a small, dark mole on her neck that was just visible under her hair. Her tits weren't huge, but they came to a nice pointed nipple. Her stomach was flat with a pierced belly button; the jewel hung down about a quarter inch and rested just above her small, red panties.

I looked at her for a while. Then I turned the page and put the paper in front of me and focused my attention on eating my dinner.

After about twenty minutes, one of the managers came upstairs and poked his head into the cafeteria. "Grindley. Shouldn't you be back downstairs yet? There are still plenty of cages to work." He wore thick, black glasses and took his job far too seriously. He was tall, but very thin. His hair had started to go a bit on top. Not many people were tall enough to have noticed, but I had noticed.

"I'll be down in ten. I'm just finishing my food."

"You should have eaten quicker. You'll be late, unless you leave now!"

It's true; I probably was going to be late.

"I'll come down in a minute." I pulled up my paper to block him from view.

"Fine if that's how you're playing it, Grindley." He walked out. I put the paper down. Waited a couple more minutes then I headed back down onto the shop floor. The second I came into the back area, he was there. Red slip in hand.

"Eighteen thirty-three, Grindley! You're late." He handed me the slip. A red slip was a warning. There were three categories you were judged on: time keeping, teamwork and customer care. I was on amber on teamwork, but red on customer care and time keeping. If you got reds in all categories they would let you go.

He looked pleased as he handed me the red slip. "That's an hour's pay docked for taking too long on your break."

Out of today's ten-hour shift, I was now looking at been paid for eight hours of that, minus my unpaid break. I put the slip in my pocket; walked round to get another cage out of the chiller. Then I took the slip out of my pocket and threw it on the floor and kicked it off under a pile of grocery cages.

7

When I got back home, Louise was asleep. She had left me a dinner out. I walked into the kitchen and lifted the silver foil that was covering my meal. Chips, ham and beans. I put it in the microwave. She had left me a glass of water out. I picked it up and sipped at it. The microwave pinged at me. I put down the water and went to the microwave, pulled out my food and touched it in the middle. It was still cold. I stirred the plate into one big mush and put it back in for another minute. I picked up the water and poured it down the sink. I opened the cupboard under the sink and pulled out a bottle of whiskey. I poured myself a good two fingers and threw it back. It gave a sweet, warming sensation all the way into my stomach. I poured another solid two fingers and mixed it with water. Placed the bottle carefully back away under the sink and picked my food out of the microwave.

I sat down in the living room and watched music channels for a while as I ate my food. Once I had eaten, I sat and sipped at my whiskey. I changed the channels a few times, scrolling through. I went onto a few of the dirtier channels and watched Babestation. I watched as they rubbed their breasts against the pink, fluffy carpet they had on set. One of their more popular moves was to bounce their arse quickly and set it wobbling round. I liked that. I held my drink in one hand and my other hand was resting on my cock. I was getting hard. I turned the TV off, necked my drink and walked into the bedroom.

I took off my clothes and got in under the covers next to Louise. I cuddled up behind her, spooning her. I swept back her hair and kissed at her neck a little. She wasn't awake. Then I reached down and pulled aside her panties. I began playing with her pussy, rubbing it. She still didn't seem to be awake, but she was getting wet and was making tiny sounds at the end of her breathing. I grabbed my cock and rubbed it up against her pussy trying to find a way in. Then I slid into her; she moaned a little. I penetrated in a few times and then started to fondle her breasts. She kept her eyes closed but turned her head to kiss me. I kept thrusting harder and faster until I was full on smashing it. She was screaming in one, long continuous groan: "OhhhhhhhhhGodddddddddYeahhhhhhhhhh!"

"Yeah, bitch, you like that?"

"Oh, God, yeah, yeah!"

"What do you like? Tell me what you like."

"I love your fucking cock in my pussy. Oh, Fuck ME, FUCK ME!"

I hit it as hard as I could. I was getting short on breath. I took in a big lungful of air and gave it a huge effort. Right as I was going dizzy from oxygen deprivation, I shot myself into her. I stroked a few more times after to savour the sensation. I pulled out and grabbed some wank rag I kept beside the bed. I wiped myself down, threw her a piece, and then lay to settle. She came over and positioned herself on me.

"That was fucking amazing."

"Yeah. It was alright," I replied.

She rubbed her hand over my chest and kissed at my neck. After a while, her hand stopped moving and I felt her head get heavy on my shoulder. I reached over her, and then rolled her off me onto her back. Then I came back to my side of the bed and went to sleep.

8

A few days later, I got a call. The guy on the other side was from the supermarket.

"Hello?" I answered.

"Grindley?"

"Yeah."

"It's Rich. We need you for overtime on DotCom."

"I don't wanna do it."

"You have to do it, Grindley."

"No I don't, why do I?"

"Because if you don't do it, I'll mark you down red on

teamwork."

"Oh come on. Argh. When is it?"

"Friday morning, 5am."

"Shit, I can't do that. I don't finish my shifts until midnight."

"You know what'll happen if I mark you down to red on teamwork, Grindley."

"Fine. I'll fucking do it."

"Good chap. See you early on Friday."

9

On the Friday morning, I got out of bed at 5am. I hadn't bothered to get undressed from work the previous evening. I stood straight up as I threw the covers off myself and doubled them up over Louise. Everything I needed was still right next to the bed, including a half drunk beer. I picked it up and pressed it to my lips. I threw my head back as if necking pills and opened my throat. The beer went down easy; better than any hangover cure. I grabbed keys and wallet and headed for work.

I pulled into an empty car park. I left my car right outside the store entrance to piss off the managers. I swiped in at 5.15am, late and loosing pay. But I didn't want to be there anyway. I headed through the store towards DotCom. There was nobody about, not one person to report to and nobody to tell me what to do. I left there and made my way up to the cafeteria. The night crews were still on. Their shift finished at 7am. They were sat making themselves breakfast. I grabbed a plate and got myself some food. The cafeteria was unmanned. There was no one to pay; it was like a free for all. I grabbed myself some beans and toast. Sat down with a coffee and started eating in the quietest corner I could find.

One of the delivery drivers came over and sat with me.

"Rough night?" he asked.

"Damn right," I said. "I only left this place five hours ago. I only got to bed three hours ago, and I'm still owed a morning dump."

"I've got something that makes the day go a little easier if you fancy a hit?"

He held out a small hip flask. I picked up my coffee and took a sip. Then I moved it slowly under the table and gave him a nod to top me up. I sat there drinking for a while. The crowd started to disburse and head back to work.

"What time is it, buddy?"

I looked at my watch. "Just approaching 6am."

"Wow, shit. We better get back down. Store Manager

comes in around now."

I drank the rest of my coffee and headed downstairs. The warehouse was full of bodies now, frantically doing work. I went back towards DotCom and picked up a little scooter-trolley. We had lists of the shopping people had ordered online from the previous day. I had numbers and locations written on a small PDA along with stock name and volume. It was basically just doing about twenty people's shopping at once. I walked around grabbing things off the shelves. Number 23, location B,2, mascarpone cheese, quantity, 1. I reached out. There was no mascarpone cheese. I was supposed to give them a different brand or nearest substitute. I threw a block of value cheddar in and kept walking.

One of the people's shopping list I found hilarious: condoms, lube, candles, matches, olive oil and string. I put it all in the basket. This was probably a fairly proud person not wanting to come and be seen buying this shit. I'd be proud if I was buying that stuff - well apart from the jonnies - I hate wearing them.

I kept working. It was a tedious task. Every once in a while a manager would grab me and ask me how I was getting on. Where was I at? How much was left to do? I just kept walking around the store picking things up, filling my tray and then getting a new tray as I dropped my full one off in the back. I maintained a pretty good buzz through the entire shift.

10

At quitting time, I got changed into my training gear. I had to go and do something. I knew I had to train. It was the only thing that gave me a reason to be living. It was my lottery, my chance at being something more then everybody else. I looked at the clock. Time was ticking on. I was tired. I text Coach: 'Not gonna make training today. Will go for run now between shifts.' I hit send.

I headed out of the supermarket and followed a route towards the city centre. I ran down this long road, there were a few bars and pubs. I kept a steady pace about myself. It was still cold out. There was a fine rain that was drenching me. I ran past dog walkers and students. I decided to play a game with myself. I was going to run street lamp to street lamp. I'd run one hard and then jog to the next, then hard again. I did it for a while; it really ramped up the workout. I was breathing heavily. I stopped and started to head back towards the supermarket. Now my game was jog one, walk one. It was less of a game and more an act of survival. I was half way back to work and I'd been well over an hour, at this point I was on jog one walk two.

I passed one of the pubs that I'd seen on my way out; when I was full of energy. I walked in, ordered a pint of lager. I had no cash on me so I gave him my card. I never liked paying on my card. It wouldn't always go through. As I sat and looked at the chip and pin machine I was thinking: 'When did I last get paid? What have I bought this month?' Then the machine beeped at me and I snapped back in to my barstool. It was going through. I entered my four-digit pin. The barman released my drink to me. I sat there and supped back the refreshing pint. There were peanuts on the bar and crisps in small bowls. I grabbed at them as I drank. I totalled the two bowls. Then I necked what was left of my pint. I stood up, turned to walk towards the door, and then turned back a quarter twist.

"Cheers."

I shouted back. It was intended for the barman, but said so half-heartedly as nothing more than at best a mild courtesy.

I walked back out into the cold rain. I was through with running now. I walked, hands in pockets, back towards the supermarket. I was knackered. When I arrived back at work, I swiped in. Walked around for a while; then I found a big, blue bag that was used to put waste cardboard in. I went to the back of the warehouse behind the tall stacks of bread. I sat in the blue bag pulled it up over my head, and went to sleep.

When I woke it was around dinnertime; the warehouse was quiet. Everyone who could leave early on Friday nights did. It was just me and the rest of the minimum wagers. I went out onto the shop floor. I just liked being out there on Fridays. It was full of single mothers who had just dropped their kids on fathers. There were sexy, female businesswomen picking up food as they relocated their office to their homes for the weekend. Girls dressed up to hit the town all weekend. They would be buying the cheap booze to get themselves loaded before heading out.

I picked up a couple of stacks of meat and stayed on the shop floor. I loved the sexy suits, the slutty girls and those milfs on their few nights away from responsibility. It was the older ones that would usually flirt. The young girls cared too much about the uniform; too much about working in a supermarket; they were repulsed by my status.

This one woman came round dressed in a tight blouse and a skirt that rested just above her knees. She looked old; her hair was a dark brown: dyed. Her legs were silky smooth, tanned and sexy. I followed her casually around the store. She kept crossing back on herself. Her arse looked tight and tidy. From the waist down, she was as young and sexy as the eighteen to twenty-five year olds that were dressed to reveal for their night on the town.

As the night went on, it became quieter in store. I walked down the beers, wines and sprits' aisle. I picked up a four pack of beer. I went to the self-serve checkout and bought them. Then I headed upstairs for a long break. Nobody was really about; there were only a handful of staff on and at this time of the night most of them were as bitter as me. I elected not to forfeit wages by signing out for my break - just so long as nobody found out. I went upstairs sat down and drank my beer.

11

A few weeks went by with nothing much eventful happening, until one Tuesday, Louise came home from work with a redundancy letter. I skipped training the next morning so I could sit with her. She worked at a clothing store as a customer sales advisor. She was coming up to a year in the job. If she had stayed working there a few more weeks, they wouldn't have been able to get rid of her without paying a redundancy package. All the firms did it. The supermarket wouldn't make me permanent for the same reason. They always want to be able to terminate you instantly with no reprieve.

I opened a bottle of wine on Wednesday morning. Instead of regular breakfast, we had a full English. We drained the wine and fucked on the sofa. Things didn't seem that bad when we fucked. I didn't worry about where we'd find money. She didn't seem to worry either. It was just simple. We fucked a lot that week. I found it so draining. I would come back late from work, tired and aching. Louise would just pounce on me and pound me. I told her if she wanted to keep fucking me three times a day then she would have to go on top. She did, but every now and then she would complain.

"Let me bend over and fuck me?" It was never so much

a question as an instruction. When I told her no, she would start crying or get angry. I always preferred it when she got angry, at least then she would sit on top of me and fuck me again. If she cried, I always felt guilty and would put more effort into the fuck.

By the end of the month, we were flat broke. I was a wreck from training, work and Louise's three fucks a day. We had no money. Louise could find no job. She was on the dole but had only just started to get payments through. We couldn't make the rent that month. I got an eviction note from the landlord: 'Please vacate the property within the next 24 hours. Pay the months' rent or we will seize your possessions.'

I took out a payday lone and paid the landlord. He was a pretty decent guy. I never once addressed him by name, but he did tell me what it was - I just wasn't listening. He didn't accept the full amount for the month. He took £300 and left me with £150.

12

We spent the night in my car. I'd left most of our belongings in the flat. There wasn't much anyway. I had in a bag my uniform for the supermarket; a couple of training clothes and spikes and a pair of jeans with a t-shirt and a smart shirt. Louise packed all her clothes into two holdalls and left them in her car.

I had the slightly bigger car. It was an S reg Astra, 1999. It was in racing green; had done about 150,000 miles and was a total banger. Warning lights came on whenever I drove it for more than a mile. I had to constantly top up the coolant system with water- there was obviously a leak somewhere. Louise had a small 205, a K reg, and I don't know what year that is. We'd bought it for £350 when she got her job. It worked out more cost effective than getting the bus everywhere.

That day whilst I was out training and working, Louise was touring the local shelters trying to find us somewhere else to sleep. She met me that night in the supermarket car park. There was just my car with our bags in the back and her.

"I've sold my car."

"Okay," I replied. "That's good. I guess you don't really need it now anyway."

Her eyes were welling up with tears. "No. No, I'm not going to need it." I looked at her and I felt a gruelling emptiness in the pit of my stomach.

"I'm going home. To my mother's. I've sold the car. Bought a train ticket. Here." She held out an envelope to me. "I want you to have this." I took it and opened it. "That's what's left of the money from the car." There was just over £125 in there.

"I can't." I gave it back to her. She refused.

"No, I don't need it. You do. I want you to have it."

"When is your train?"

"Not until tomorrow. I'm getting the 11.06."

"I'll take you there."

She smiled and hugged into me close; she was crying. I felt like I'd just lost everything. It had only just dawned on me how low I'd fallen. Of course, she was leaving me. I was making her sleep in a car.

We moved the car to the darkest corner of the car park. Climbed into the back seats and got under a blanket. She lay with her head on my chest. I could feel every one of my own heartbeats. I kissed her softly, sweetly and gently. My hands flowed over her body, following the motion of her contours. She turned slightly to face me; she was now laid on top. Her hand went down to my cock and started to rub it. She pulled down her jeans and slid me inside of her. We rocked smoothly, lightly stroking inside her.

I softly whispered to her, "You know I..."

She smiled back, kissed me and said, "I love you."

I lay there most of the night. So aware of her: of her face, freckles and most of all her scent. I'd never realised just how beautiful she was.

13

In the morning, we decided to walk to the station. It was a couple of miles but I was low on fuel and it was the last time that we had together. We walked holding hands as we each dragged her bags. When we got near to the station, I sent her off on her own briefly. I pointed her down Greek Street towards the station; I gave her both bags in case I wasn't there in time to see her off. I wouldn't say goodbye though. I knew I had to make it up to her.

I ran into the city centre to the shops. I went straight into the jewellery shop and I took out the envelope of cash. A woman came over to me.

"Can I help you with anything, sir?"

"Yes, you can." I gave her the money. "I've got this and a few quid more if I need it. A woman that's been so good to me, probably the best woman I've known, is leaving. I want to do something nice for her. So she remembers me, so she knows I care for her."

The woman looked into the envelope and counted the cash. "How much extra did you say you had?"

I emptied my wallet on the table: £135. I put a tenner back in my wallet for food and gave her the rest. "Here."

She went away and brought back a beautiful bracelet

and ring. "These are within your price range. What do you think she'd prefer?"

I didn't know. I hadn't known anything about her at all. I had just taken her for granted all this time.

"How much for both of them?"

"I'll give you them both for £400."

"Okay." I thought quickly then looked at my watch: 10.45. "What about my watch? If I give you the cash and my watch?"

She looked at it, then looked at me. "I'll have to ask my manager. Wait right here."

"Lady, look, please, she is getting on a train soon. I have to get there."

She pondered a while and then looked at my watch. I'd taken it off and put it on the counter. "Okay," she said. "Okay, I'll do it."

"Thank you." I grabbed the jewellery, left my watch and the cash, and ran out of the door to the station.

I made it there in time. Louise was stood on the main platform. She turned her head. She was looking around; there was concern on her face, and then she saw me and it just turned to pure glee. I ran over to her and threw my arms around her. I kissed her passionately. I gave her the jewellery.

"Here, I want you to have this. Just something to remember me by."

"Alex, you shouldn't have, you needed that money." I just smiled at her. "I love you," she said to me. It went through me like a blanket of warmth.

Her train arrived. She got onto it.

I stood and gazed admiringly at her as she powered out of the station. She was gone and, all of a sudden, I felt nothing. I needed a drink.

14

I bought a bottle of whiskey from a bargain booze store for £3.99. I had £6.01 left to survive on. I made my way back into the supermarket. I went to my locker; it now had a few different changes of clothes in. I took a good hit from the bottle and I went out onto the shop floor to work. I worked right through; I stopped for a toilet break and to take another swig. As I came back down, there was one of the managers, Rich. He looked at me trying to find a reason to write me up.

"Grindley, come with me. You've been randomly selected for a staff search."

I followed him into the search room.

"Turn out your pockets."

"Wait," I said. "What about my representative?"

It was a known fact that you'd only ask for a representative if you had something that you shouldn't.

"What ya got, Grindley?" he smiled a gruesome smile as he rubbed his hands together expectantly.

"Nothing, I just want my representative."

"There isn't anyone here this late. I'll have to call someone in."

"So do it."

"You better not be fucking with me Grindley."

He went and called a rep from the union. He locked the door and left the camera on in the interrogation room. It was supposed to be a hold for shoplifters but I'd never seen anyone but staff locked in there since I'd started. I sat in the room for over an hour. I moved my chair against the wall in the corner, so I could rest my head back. I closed my eyes. Every few minutes, Rich would look in through the window; see my eyes closed and knock sharply on the glass. I didn't open my eyes at first and he just kept on knocking. Then I opened them and looked at him. He stopped and walked away. A few minutes later, we'd play the same game.

Finally, the rep came. Rich brought in a police constable too. We did it all by the book. The PC took charge of the search.

"Name?"

"Alex Grindley."

"Age?"

"Twenty-five."

"Right, Mr Grindley, please empty your pockets. Place all loose items on the table."

"You're for it now, Grindley," Rich chirped up from the background.

I emptied my pockets and saw the disappointment on Rich's face.

"Thank you, Mr Grindley. Now if I could ask you to face the wall and place both palms on the wall and spread your legs."

I did it; I turned my head to look at Rich as he looked increasingly bothered by what was happening. He caught me looking. I shot him a smile and a wink.

"Thank you, Mr Grindley." The police officer took a step back. "He's got nothing on him."

"No. No! He's hidden it."

My union rep finally spoke up. "He's been searched and cleared. Feel free to go back to work, Alex."

I stood up and walked out. I picked up my items as I went. I walked until I found a flat table; then I stopped. I tucked my shirt back into my trousers. I put my diary, pen and a fiver all back into my pockets.

"Grindley!" Rich was marching towards me. "I need you for DotCom overtime. Tomorrow and all next week at 5am."

"That's fine. Cheers, Rich." Then I walked away.

By the end of the night, I was hungry. I'd not eaten properly for two days, and I'd not had any food that day at all. I slept on a sofa in the canteen. It wasn't warm so I kept my work fleece on. I kept getting woken up at various points in the evening when the night staff came up for their breaks. I had a quick look every time I was woken to see if there was any unmanned food lying about. There wasn't.

The canteen started to get busy at 5am. I was woken up by the same guy that had slipped me the whiskey a few weeks back. He had his backpack with him; he brought out a small hip flask.

"I can see you need a solid hit today."

"Damn right."

He went and grabbed some coffee mugs, minus the coffee. Then he poured me a full mug of whiskey. I sat there and drank. As I drank, my appetite began to fade. I wasn't as aware of the hunger for a while.

"It's Dale, mate, my name."

"Alex," I replied.

"You got the time, Alex?"

"No, mate, not got a watch right now."

"Want one?"

"What, you're gonna give me a watch?"

"Sure, I got a few in the van. I keep hold of a few things on the deliveries. I'll sell you it?"

"I've not got any cash, mate."

"Oh fuck it, you can have it then."

"Seriously?"

"Yeah, it didn't cost me owt. And every guy needs to catch a break at some point."

We didn't say too much after that. I was mainly scanning the room to see if I could grab some food from somewhere. About 5.45 the canteen was unmanned. I walked over and grabbed bacon, eggs, beans and toast. Piled it on a plate and took it to the men's toilets. I held my cup of whiskey tightly between my knees with my plate resting on my left arm. I held it close to my face and just shovelled the food into my mouth. I ate it quickly, and it filled a gap. Once I'd finished, I felt fine, it was almost like my two days of forced fasting hadn't happened at all. I sat there and dropped a solid morning shit as I finished my drink.

My time on the shop floor went quickly. I was doing the shopping for the online customers again. Instead of doing one list at a time like they tried to make me do, I took a handful of them and set about doing them all at once. It meant I wasn't going back and forth across the entire store so many times. I got the workload done significantly quicker. By 9am, I'd more or less finished the lot. A few items were missing. Rather than replace all of them with substitutes, I just didn't put them in. I left my trays in the delivery area out back where the drivers would pick them up; I saw a box with my name on it. I opened it and there was a watch.

I felt good. So good that I decided to go training. I needed it. I didn't want to take my car: there really wasn't much fuel in it at all. So I jogged to the track.

15

It took me about two hours to get to the track and I had to be back at work in a further three hours. My group were well into the session. I decided to jump into some runs on my own. I was plenty warmed up from the two hours of jogging. Time was against me. I ran a 300m rep as quickly as possible. They were all slugging out long, slow runs - I didn't have time for that anymore. I timed myself on my new wristwatch. It was difficult to get an exact time, as it was a clock face. I waited until the second hand came onto the '12' and then I set off. I saw as I finished that it was around the 33-34 second mark.

I sat heavy breathing. Coach was there but he didn't come over to say anything to me. I hadn't been down for a while. He was probably pissed about that. Probably pissed that I was doing my own thing at the moment.

I wandered around trying to get my recovery going. I looked to see who was around. There was a new girl who I'd not seen before. She had long blonde hair. She had a bottle tan all over. I was staring at her; she caught my gaze and looked away. I decided to keep looking her way. A few seconds later, she looked back, I guess assuming that I would have looked away but I hadn't. This time she looked away quickly but laughed to herself. I saw her look back over to me smiling. She cocked her head to one side sharply, signalling me over.

"Do you stare at a lot of girls like that?"

"Only the pretty ones."

She smiled again. She was smoking hot: wearing long Lycra, her bum just popped out. She was a cute, petite girl - big tits for her size. She had quite a square face, but perfectly symmetrical. She was gorgeous.

"What ya got today?" I picked up the conversation trying to engage her.

"Nothing much. Just a bit of a workout." She paused for

a short while. "What you up to?"

"I'm just running a couple of 300's." I kept looking straight into her eyes; they were a mixture of blue and green. "I'm Alex."

"Hi, Alex." She giggled to herself.

"Don't I get your name?"

"You might, if you're lucky."

"Well, what is it?"

She picked up her phone and fiddled with it. "I'm going to Tiger Tiger tonight. If I see you there, maybe I'll tell you."

"Okay, cool. How will I find you?'

"I'll be in the queue around 1ish. We're going walkabout first for pre-drinks."

"I'll see you there."

"Sure." She said it as if I wasn't going to be there.

"No seriously. I'll be there."

She smiled and then walked away. I was pumped. I was excited. I went to go and do another run. I was so full of energy. I waited on the 300m start mark for my second hand to reach the '12' mark. When it did I set off. I felt each foot push the ground away. It felt so slow in my mind, but I knew I was moving quickly. Each ground contact was landing directly under my body; my shins were striking the ground around forty-five degrees angle, and then my body started to rise upwards. My ground contacts became quicker and my shin angle more open. My arms were moving powerfully by my side driving me forward. I ran onto the first curve and felt my stride shorten slightly, but it increased in speed. Half way around the corner, I started to really push forward. As the curve opened up onto the straight, I opened my stride again. My head held straight, looking in front of me. I could feel my legs tiring now, but it wasn't enough to stop me. My knee lift became less, but my arms took up the slack, they came in to keep the power going. I crossed the line and looked at my watch: 31-32 maybe.

As I walked around afterwards, dealing with the incredible pain of the runs, I couldn't see any sign of the mystery girl. I caught my breath and then headed back to work. Even though I was fucked from the workout, I ran to get there in time. I felt like shit by the time I made it back to the supermarket.

I bought a bottle of value beer for 99p and made my way up to my locker. I drained the beer and threw on some work clothes. I kept myself looking busy at work, but the whole time I was just watching the clock, waiting for midnight for my shift to end. I didn't take a break right until the end of my shift. At 11.30pm, I took my break. I hit the showers, and got dressed into some casual clothes. At midnight, my break ended and so did my shift. I clocked out and started to walk towards the city centre.

16

It was just before 1am when I got to the club. I saw her with a group of girls in the line waiting to get in. I walked over.

"Oh my God! You came!" She was amazed. She was leaning on her friends to stay up; they were all pretty smashed. I stood there in the line with her for a while. Then she turned to me.

"I got a bottle of vodka at home. You wanna just go to mine, get pissed, listen to music and fuck?"

"Hell, yeah."

We jumped out of the line and walked a little while to a taxi stand. The taxi driver opened his window just a little and she peered in and said her address. I couldn't quite make it out. We got into the back seat. As soon as I sat down, she started making out with me. Her lips were soft. She had a sweet taste of wine and mixers on her breath. I soaked it in. I used one of my hands to run it across her stomach. It was sexy and flat. There was a little scar where she had once had a belly button ring; I rubbed my index finger over it softly and then went back to firmly running my hands over her chest and abdomen.

We got to her house. It was a straight fiver for the taxi, so I paid him. I had just 2p left in my wallet. We made our way inside. She grabbed the vodka from the kitchen and two glasses. I followed her up the stairs into the bedroom. I took the bottle off her as she kissed me again. Then she bounced off me, biting her bottom lip and taking off her top. She was wearing a deep purple bra with black lace. She threw the top on the floor, turned and walked over to the CD player. She put on some classic rock tunes.

"Hell fucking yeah!" I said.

She smiled at me, then walked quickly towards me and jumped on me. I caught her and fell backwards onto the bed. Her legs were straggling me. She kissed me, then sat up and pulled off her bra. Her tits were great, nipples sharp and pointing. I sat up and took off my top, then extended my tongue and licked her nipples, she moaned a little and started grinding me through her leggings. I turned her over so she was lying underneath me; then I began to pull off her leggings. She quickly got to work on my jeans. Undoing the belt; then pulling them down and exposing my hard cock. She took it in her mouth and began moving her head up and down on it. Then she worked the tongue, licking the length. She pushed me back over so I was on my back. She began to rotate herself round. She lowered her hips and force-fed me her pussy. As I licked it, she got more and more into sucking my cock. She sat herself up and sat right back on my face. I could hardly breathe, but I was pushing my tongue wherever I could. She grabbed her arse with either hand and spread it.

"Lick it. I want you to lick my arse."

I pushed my tongue as deep in there as I could. Then I circulated it around and pushed it back in. She loved it; she was moaning louder and louder. She kept pushing her arse harder into me. As she came up off me slightly, I grabbed some precious air and used my strength to throw her off me. She caught herself on all fours and bounced on the bed. I came round behind her and pushed my cock up to her backside. The saliva made it easy to glide into her shit hole. I worked it hard. It was tighter than any pussy I'd had. I didn't want to push it too deep so I stroked only down to mid-length.

"Oh yeah, fuck that arsehole. I love it!"

As she continued to moan and bounce back into my cock, I ventured deeper: I was fucking her arse hard. I kept pounding in her. She started rubbing her pussy and fingering herself. I could feel her fingers moving in her pussy and rubbing against my cock; it was so sensitive, so tight. I smashed into her as hard as I could and came. As I pulled out cum dripped from her: it was a mixture of light brown shit. My cock too had a light brown coating of shit. I wiped it on the bed sheets then grabbed the bottle of vodka. I poured two good portions and handed one over to her.

"I love been fucked hard."

"Good to know." I took a good hit of the vodka.

"Yeah. I thought you'd like that. You look like you'd be up for just about anything."

"Well with you being kind enough to let me at your intimate areas, I think it's only polite that I take requests."

She smiled and then took a solid few gulps of the vodka. I followed suit and necked my glass. I poured another two large glasses of the clear liquid.

"So what is your name?"

"Lisa."

We left the music playing and drank. She fell asleep; naked, sprawled across me. I had another glass of vodka before I turned the light off and fell asleep.

I woke at 6am; late for work. I got up quietly, took the bottle of vodka, left Lisa a note and then set off for work. I recognized the house in daylight; it wasn't far away from the supermarket.

17

I spent a couple of weeks staying at Lisa's place. Not every night. Some nights I'd stay at the supermarket and sleep in the canteen. Other nights I'd spend in the pub round the corner; then on to some bars in the city centre. I started to get some rhythm going. I was even turning up to training once or twice a week; after I'd managed to stop doing the extra work on DotCom.

I'd even paid off my payday loan. I'd started to get some money together. I was giving Lisa little bits of cash. I'd buy the drinks for our nights of filth and chuck in a couple of quid for rent and bills.

I kept it going for five weeks without addressing what was going on between us. Then, on the Saturday evening, she just came out with it.

"Are we together, Alex?"

"Well, yeah, kinda."

"What do you mean kinda?"

"Well, you know. I mean I'm not fucking anyone else."

"You're not fucking anyone else? What the fuck is that supposed to mean?"

"No, no. I didn't mean anything bad with it."

"What the fuck, Alex? You're not fucking anyone else. But you fucking want to don't you?"

"Babe. Every guy sees a hot chick and wants to bang it. It doesn't mean a thing."

"You know what, Alex. Just get the fuck out."

I knew what I'd said that was wrong. If I'd only said

what I knew I was supposed to, I'd have been sorted.

I went to work. I worked my shift then went and hit the bars. I drank heavily. I didn't want to go back to see her. I decided to give her some room to cool off.

18

That Sunday evening, I went back to the house. It was full of people; there was music blasting out from open windows and doors. I walked in squeezing past people. I went into the kitchen and grabbed a beer. I walked around bouncing off people. I was half looking for Lisa, but I didn't want her to see me yet.

I drained that beer and grabbed another two. I shot one back and drained the bottle. Then I carried the second and supped it heavily. I managed to work my way into a drinking game round the dining table. I didn't much care for social interactions. But I was thankful of the chair and having drinks thrust before me.

We started out playing 'Asshole': it was some game with cards. I got dealt cards and had to get rid of them to the player on my left whilst the girl to my right was doing the same to me. I wasn't good. I kept missing additional rules like putting my thumb on the table. They kept dropping bottles of beer in front of me.

"Drink, drink, drink, drink!"

I was able to down them with relative ease. It caused

the crowd to break into song.

"Down in one Zulu Warrior, down in one Zulu Warrior!"

They followed that up with an old football chant that they'd turned into university slagging banter.

"When I was just a young boy, I asked my mother what should I be. Should I be Uni? Should I be Met? And here's what she said to me; wash your mouth out, son, and get your father's gun, to shoot the Uni scum, the Uni scum."

We sat drinking and playing games for a while. Some of the girls in the game had started taking clothes off rather than doing drinking forfeits. The girl to my left was wearing a pair of blue French panties and a matching bra. I kept placing my hand on her leg. It felt good. Soft and smooth. She had great legs. I'd thought before she was down to her bare minimum that she was fit. She had come in a denim mini-skirt. I wanted to have a good look at her legs from the start.

As I moved my hand ever higher up her leg, there was nothing going on in my pants. I knew I was too drunk to make it work. Still, I enjoyed feeling her legs. But not quite as much as I enjoyed the seemingly endless supply of beer.

I left the games as they started to patter out. Nobody was drinking heavily anymore. The songs were slurred and even the influx of drinks got sloppy. I walked back to the kitchen. The party was much less active now. People close to passing out all over the place. They were laid across cars on the street; across the drive, the walls, sofas: everywhere. Those few that were still active were draping themselves over one another. I grabbed another beer and went back to look for Lisa. I walked up to her room. She was laid on the bed with some guy.

"Alex? What are you doing here?"

I looked at her. And the drink replied for me. "I'm here to break up with you. Truth is, I'm just not attracted to you since you've gained weight."

I walked out. I made a stop in the kitchen and grabbed a bottle of whiskey and a pack of beers. I could hear her behind me, calling me. I got out onto the drive way and then stopped. I turned to face her, she looked shocked. Tears had fucked up her makeup.

"What do you mean you're breaking up with me?"

"You know, Lisa. You're such a fucking whore. You'd make a lot more money if you'd do it professionally."

Then I walked off drinking the beers.

19

I took the next day off training and went to an estate agent. I picked a beat-up part of town and walked into what looked like the most run down place there. I walked in and this middle-aged woman was sat behind the desk. She didn't seem to have much going on. There weren't many properties listed.

"Can I help you?"

"Yeah. I need somewhere to sleep tonight and probably for a while. What sort of places do you have?"

She looked at me. I could tell she wanted to ask about my price range, employment and all that but, to her credit, she didn't. I was willing to bet that she needed the business. She pulled a few bits of paper from her drawer and showed me the flats. They were all pretty shit. One of them was furnished.

"I'll take a look at that one, please."

She got a set of keys and then walked me round the corner to the flat. We walked in through a shared door that had been left open. She closed it behind her. We walked up to the third floor. The door had dints down the front and against the frame.

"We had to get the last guy out with force," she explained, as she pointed out the crowbar damage.

We walked in and she began to talk me through it. I didn't really listen. I walked into the kitchen and put Lisa's whiskey on the table. I had previously concealed it in my coat pocket. The flat had a bed, a sofa, a table and a crapper.

"I'll take it."

"Really? Well, that's great. I have the paper work here if you'd like to go through it? It's £33 per week and you take care of your own bills. I will need the first week in advance."

"Cash okay?"

I pulled out around £100; her face illuminated.

"Are you always going to be able to pay in cash?"

"If it helps the both of us I can."

"It would help us. I'll lower the price to £30 a week for you if it's cash?"

"Cash is fine then."

I opened the whiskey and looked in the cupboard for a glass. I found a couple of tea stained mugs. I gestured to see if she wanted a drink.

"Okay, why not? It would be rude not to celebrate your new place."

I poured a couple of good portions of whiskey and gave her the mug. She sat on the sofa and started going through the paperwork, occasionally sipping at the whiskey. I sat myself close next to her and kept topping up the drinks as we went through the tedious signing and initialling.

As I was drinking, I noticed that she wasn't a bad looking woman. A bit chubby maybe. Good style though. Wearing a pencil skirt without any tights on. Her legs were quite tanned.

"You have some really nice tanned legs."

"Oh, thank you. I go on the sun beds now and then."

"Oh really? Are you a white bits' girl?"

"You're terrible. Well, if you want to know, I have no white bits, this is an all over tan."

"I don't believe you. You'll have to prove it to me."

She smiled and bashfully opened her blouse a little. She pulled back her bra strap and showed that there were no tan lines there.

"That's not good enough. How do I know that you don't just have a strapless bra on?"

"Okay then."

She took a good hit of the whiskey then undid the rest of her blouse and took off her bra. Her tits were nice, they were quite small, but I could see how the extra weight she carried had added to their size. I reached out my hand and felt one. She closed her eyes and exhaled heavily throwing her head back. I leant in and started kissing her neck. She started undoing my jeans and I moved down to kiss her breasts.

She got my fly open and grabbed my cock, pulling it out. Then she went down and started working at it with her mouth and hands. She would bob up and down whilst her hand was doing light rotations on the shaft. It felt good. I reached out for the whiskey and took a solid hit. Then I gave her a solid hit as I came in her mouth. She pulled up and gipped, she spat out my come in the mug. I handed her the bottle and she took another long pull.

I signed the rest of the paperwork and she left. I took a nap in my new bed. Then I got up and headed off to work.

20

Weeks went by and Christmas came. I didn't do anything special. The supermarket made me take a day's holiday for Christmas. I didn't want to.

I sat at home and watched the TV drinking beer. I didn't have anything in for a Christmas dinner. I ate a jam sandwich and then washed that down with a couple more beers. I sat in and watched the Queen's speech. It was all about taking care of one another; being there for friends, family and neighbours. I toasted to her and necked the beer.

It was starting to get dark and I'd run out of beers. I decided to do something useful with my day. I put on my training gear and I went out into the street. I started jogging towards the track. When I got there, it was dark and all locked up. There were no floodlights and I could hardly see a thing.

I climbed the fence. It seemed much higher once I had reached the top. I fell over the other side and landed on my backside. I started to run round the track and do a warm up. I stretched out. It wasn't that cold for the middle of winter. There was no snow or ice.

I put my spikes on and started to run some fast, short distances. I ran about four or five 100 meters back to back. I felt quick. I had managed to put in at least one or two good sessions a week recently, and I thought it was starting to show.

I spent a couple of hours there just running. Getting out was easy. The turn-style would always open from trackside. I walked out. On my way home, I passed a few pubs. I walked into one of the more lively places and I took myself to the bar.

"Two bottles of red wine, please?"

"House?"

"House is fine."

He brought them over and uncorked them both. I paid him. Left the glasses on the bar and took the bottles. I walked out onto the street and began to drink one of the bottles as I made my way back to the apartment.

21

I worked as usual the next week. On New Year's Eve, I was working till midnight. There were hardly any of us in store. I got a cage out from the back. I had plenty more that I should have worked. There was only one manager in, and she had just got engaged at Christmas to her boyfriend. She had spent all night upstairs in the managers' office on the phone. I hadn't seen her once.

There were no customers and no cars in the car park. The store was dead.

I put my cage next to the deli counter. A new girl had started working there at Christmas. She was so beautiful. 'Deli Girl' I called her. She looked around 18 years old. She looked great in work trousers. As she would move about the place, the trousers would cling to her sexy figure. She didn't have curves. She was pretty small really.

I synchronized my breaks to coincide with hers. I would sit with my coffee just looking at her. She was reading the paper. She kept glancing up at me; then would pull the paper up to cover her face as she made out she was reading. Each time the paper would drop, I could make out her glowing cheeks. She caught me looking again and again she blushed, trying to hide it behind the paper.

At the end of break, I again positioned myself close to where she was working. I couldn't take my eyes off her.

The night dragged. At 23.55 everyone that was in store gathered by the clock out gate. We all had our coats on. The clock on the wall was getting closer to midnight. I didn't know who started it but I heard it, then more of them, then I joined in.

"10, 9, 8, 7, 6, 5, 4, 3, 2, 1. Happy New Years!"

I was queuing up behind Deli Girl to swipe out. She clocked out then turned straight into me without realising. We looked at one another for a moment: it seemed to last forever. Then I just kissed her lightly on the lips. I didn't even know I was doing it - it just happened. She kissed back a little, but didn't say anything.

"Are you doing anything tonight?" I asked.

"No," she replied.

"Do you wanna go somewhere?"

"We won't get in anywhere at this time."

"I know a place we can go. If you fancy?"

"Okay." She smiled at me as she said it. There wasn't any doubt or hesitation in her voice.

"Great. Do you know my car outside? The Astra?" She nodded. "Meet me there. I'll be two minutes."

I swiped out and then turned to go back into the store. I

went to the beers wines and spirits and was looking along them quickly. What to get? Wine? Beer? Spirits? I grabbed a bottle of Southern Comfort. I paid and exited through the front door of the store.

She was waiting by my car. I opened it up and got in. We were both still dressed in our uniforms. I started driving towards the city centre.

She reached into my lap and pulled out the bottle.

"Open it," I said.

She did and took a good long pull, swallowed and then coughed a little.

"Bit strong?" I joked.

"No, I fucking love it."

She took another long pull and this time didn't struggle with the aftertaste.

I drove through the city, past the clubs. No more than 300 yards away from the drunken bustle there was a small roundabout, in the centre was a memorial. I parked up on the curb of the roundabout. I got out and opened the door for Deli Girl.

"Is this it?"

"Yeah, don't knock it."

I laid my jacket on the damp grass and we sat down on

it. There was a soft glow from the orange streetlights. No cars. In the distance, we could only just hear the sound of music and sirens doing battle with one another.

I leaned over and kissed her. She kissed back and dragged her hands over my body. I moved my hand down to her trousers and undid the belt. I slid my hand down the inside of her panties. She had a serious muff. As I pushed down towards the slit, I could feel that I kept getting her pubes stuck and was pulling on them. I made it down and rubbed up and down the pussy: she was wet. I slid two fingers inside of her and lightly moved them about, in and out.

She grabbed onto my cock and thrashed at it up and down. I used my spare hand to slow her down - give her more rhythm.

We kept kissing. She started to moan a little. I took my hand off her and she started to go back to thrashing at my cock. I was getting close. I pulled my fingers out of her and pushed her head down to my cock. She opened her mouth and took it. She didn't really move much. Just kept the tip in the lips and continued to thrash harder, ripping my cock up and down. I pushed her head down. She gagged. The gaging felt good, so I kept her there. Then she came up and I pushed her back down. She came up another time. I maneuvered my hips and thrust in and out. I started to come. She moved her head away and stopped jerking my cock. I quickly took hold and finished myself off.

We sat there for a while, just drinking. I saw she was getting cold.

"I'll drive you home."

"Just drop me off at my mate's house near the supermarket."

I dropped her off. Then I drove on home. I put on some music and sat on the sofa drinking the rest of the Southern Comfort.

22

A couple of days later, I was back at training. I had just finished a 450m run and was sitting down catching my breath. The rest of the group were moving around and jogging, keeping moving. I sat and let the lactic acid take a strong hold over my muscles.

"Alex, keep moving." Coach ordered me to get up and move about. I sat there and made a feeble attempt to move. Then my phone rang and gave me reason to stop the struggle, flopping back to the ground.

"Hello?"

"Hi, is that Alex?"

"Yeah."

"Hi, Alex, my name is Jason. I'm head of the Yorkshire

athletics team."

"Okay."

"Well, basically, I was wondering if you were available to race for us this Sunday? It's an indoor meeting."

"Sunday? It's a bit short notice."

"Yeah, I'm sorry about that. I had a guy running it but he's injured. So I've just been going down a list and I've got to your name. Can you do it?"

"I'm not too sure, mate."

"Well, there is fifty quid in it for being a team member and I can double that if you win."

"Where is it?"

"It's local, it's in Sheffield. I have you down living in Leeds? I can give you a lift if you need?"

"Yeah, okay. I can do it. Where do you want me to meet you?"

"I'll pick you up from the university athletics track if that's easy for you? Say 9am?"

"Can you make it the supermarket in south Leeds?"

"Yeah, that's fine."

I hung up the phone and threw it near my bag. "Hey,

Coach!" I got up and started walking towards him.

"Alex. Congratulations on finally getting up."

"No, Coach. I have a race this weekend."

"You're actually going to race?"

"Yeah. Why wouldn't I?"

"You should race, Alex. I've wanted you to actually do a race for ages."

I made my way back to my kit and packed it up. I started to walk out.

"You not doing the second run, Alex?"

"Coach, gotta freshen up for the weekend."

23

On the Sunday, I woke early. I looked in the fridge for something to eat. There was only a beer and half of an Indian microwave meal. I opened the beer and sat to eat the cold curry. Once I finished, I went to take a dump. I sat on the shitter and squeezed out an alco shit, warm and runny. I jumped in the shower and washed my arse clean.

I went to get some kit ready for the race. I looked at what was cleanest: without food or beer stains. I found an old Puma t-shirt in green, it had a small hole under the left armpit, but for the most part was clean. I found a pair of Lycra shorts hidden away in the bottom of one of my drawers. I lifted the crotch to my nose and inhaled. They smelt clean enough. I put them on. I wasn't too bothered about my tracksuit pants. I just put on the first pair I came across. They were just laid on the floor. I went back to the kitchen. I filled a bottle with water and then I grabbed another beer out of the fridge and put it in my bag along with the water and a pair of old, battered running spikes. Then I set off to meet Jason at the supermarket.

Jason pulled up in his car. I went to get in the front seat but saw a young girl sat there so I jumped into the back seat.

"Hey, Alex, thanks for coming. This is Summer," he said, gesturing with his head towards the lass. She turned and smiled at me. She looked very young.

"Hi," I said to both of them. "Thanks for the pick-up."

"It's no problem, mate. Thanks for doing this."

Jason turned up the radio and started to drive off towards Sheffield.

24

When we got to the track, Jason parked up just round from the main entrance. I got out quickly and glanced behind me to see if they were coming. I kept walking. I could hear giggling from the car. I just ignored it and made my way to the indoor athletics track.

The indoor track was different than I had expected. It was only 200m long and had banked curves. I put my bag down and went for a jog around. I made my way past all the eventers warming up. Some of the girls in their Lycra looked fantastic. They can't have been serious athletes with arses like they had. I wanted to grab hold of them as I passed. I jogged close to one of them and let my hand dangle out so I could get a feel as I went past. Her arse brushed my hand, and I felt the softness of it; it wobbled in the collision. I jogged on passed and didn't look back.

Jason finally turned up and gave me my vest and numbers. I pinned the numbers onto the vest.

"Hey, Jason."

"Yeah?"

"When do I get my money?"

"I'll pay you cash at the end of the meeting."

"Still a hundred to win?"

"Yep. You win and I'll make it a hundred, pal."

I finished pinning my numbers on my vest and I slipped it inside my sports bag along with my shorts and spikes. I went to go and find an area to stretch and warm up.

As I warmed up, my stomach was rumbling. I hadn't eaten in a good while, and I'd hardly drunk anything to take away the hunger. I walked to the start of the race starving. They put me in lane 5. There was a tall, blonde guy in lane 4; he was the favourite to win. The fella in lane 6, just outside of me, was a short, black kid: he was representing the Midlands. I didn't look at the other competitors. They were too far away from my vision to care about.

"On your marks!"

I waited a few seconds, it felt longer, and then I moved towards my blocks. My stomach was still rumbling. All I could think about was the beer in my bag. I sat my feet into the starting blocks, and then I rocked upright and looked straight ahead of me. In my peripherals, I could see the other guys were settled. I dropped my body and head down into the crouch.

"Set!"

I pushed my back feet hard into the block plates and thrust my arse into the air.

BANG*

The gun went and I pushed out low and fast. My foot dragged along the surface of the track for the first two strides. My head was still down. I just pushed. I felt the banking on the curve turn me left and I rolled round the corner with it. As I came onto the back straight, it became clear that I was moving well. I had passed the guy in lane 6 and the favourite inside me hadn't come along side me yet. We went round the next turn and I kicked hard into the bend. As we came onto the home straight for the end of the first 200m, I passed a green tick on the track. I broke lanes and filed into the inside of the track. I was still in front. Down the back straight, I could feel my legs getting heavy and full of lactic acid. I pushed as hard as I could, but I was feeling my strides shorten, slow and my knee lift started to disappear altogether. Finally, the line came, and I was still in front as we passed it.

I looked at the clock and for the first time heard the commentator's voice in the arena, "46.34 seconds, that is the third fastest time in the world, so far this year!"

I double-checked the clock to make sure I had read it right. I had won by around a second, with the favourite coming in second place. In what was a good time of 47.25 seconds.

"Fucking awesome run Alex!" Jason screamed.

"Cheers. Can I have my money now?" I was panting as I asked the question. I walked with Jason off the track and he pulled out two, crisp fifty pound notes.

"Here you go, pal. Fucking well done."

I took the money and placed it inside my sports bag. I put my sports bag over my shoulder and walked out to the car park. I vomited. It came out of my mouth and nose as an orange paste. I used my index finger to isolate each nostril and blew out the remaining chunks. I got some on my shoe, but I managed to brush it off.

I opened my bag and pulled out a beer. I sat and drank the beer, pulling on it slowly. Then I saw Jason come out.

"Alex. C'mon pal. Get inside, we've fucking won. Beaten all the southern cunts."

I walked inside behind Jason. Summer was stood in the entrance hall.

"Go on ahead, Alex mate. I just need a quick chat with Summer." She smiled at me as if to say everything was fine. I walked back into the arena. The team was assembled in the centre of the track. I walked over to meet them.

The commentator gave the points total and declared us all the winners by 104 points to 102 - a pretty close run thing in the end. A bald man and his elderly wife shook our hands and presented the team with a bottle of champagne. I made my way to the front and collected the champagne. Everyone danced and jumped and celebrated. I took the bottle and my bag and walked outside to the car park. I managed to open the champagne by dragging the cork along a brick wall and fizzing the bottle. There wasn't much fizz to it. I found the car. No sign of Jason or Summer. I sat there and drank from the bottle.

I noticed there was a copper sat at the gate on the road. He'd been there a while looking at me. I tried to ignore him.

Jason finally came with the lass and we got into the car. No sooner than I had buckled up, the Old Bill had us surrounded. They pulled us all out of the car and put Jason and me in handcuffs. I got thrown in the back of a cop car. They drove me to the local station. I never had chance to speak with Jason or Summer.

I looked out of the window as we drove down unfamiliar streets. Each of the coppers in the front looked at me as if I was shit.

"What have I done?"

"Shut the fuck up, you filthy cunt!"

We arrived at the station and I went to the front desk in chains. They took my fingerprints. The copper brought me into the interview room. I gave my name and proof of ID. Then he sat me in there, took off my handcuffs and got me a coffee. He gave me a pen and paper.

"Here. Think about what you're gonna say to us and write it down, you piece of shit!"

He left. I looked at the paper. I picked up the pen and started doodling. I drew pictures of food. A burger, fries, a steak. I couldn't see outside of the room. I just sat there and waited.

A few hours later, the copper came back in. He was looking softer. No hard looks my way or shouting abuse.

"Sorry, mate. Didn't realise you were an innocent part to all this crap."

"What was it?"

"That guy that drove you about, he was touching up that young lass."

"What? Summer?"

"She's 14 years old. Makes me fucking sick."

"Yeah. I never liked him."

"Well, mate, you're free to go. Girl said it was the first time she'd seen you."

I walked out of the police station. It was late. I looked around. Everything was dark and shut up. I had no phone on me, just a couple of fifties. I was in Sheffield and I needed to be in Leeds. There was no way of getting back and the trains didn't run this late.

I walked to the train station anyway. It was 1am when I got there. There was some noise coming from a street not too far away. I wandered to see what it was. Maybe I could get a drink.

I walked into this club: Spearmint Rhino. It cost me a

fiver on the door. I ordered a beer; that was another fiver. I sat and watched the girls dancing. I drank my beer with a boner. One of the girls came over. She had huge tits and was wearing a leopard print bikini G-string combo. She had fantastic tits, and her ass: I wanted to part those cheeks and just live in that ass.

"Want a dance honey?"

"How much?"

"15 for a song or 30 for a private."

I gave her £30. She took my hand and walked me into the back room. She worked her ass and grinded it on me. She pulled apart her ass cheeks and wedged my cock between and bounced. She kept it going for a while. I came. She knew. She stopped.

"You're all done now then, honey?" she winked as she said it.

I wanted to fuck her hard. As she was bouncing, I'd been thinking about smashing her pussy, then pulling out and stretching her ass. Fucking it wide as she screamed. I got another beer and watched a while longer. She came back again.

"You want another dance sexy?"

"That depends."

"On what babe?"

"How sexy can you make the dance?"

"Oh babe, it's always sexy. I've got a wet, juicy pussy. I just wanna get it out and show you."

 "Do you think you could sort me out like last time?"

"Call it fifty, and I guarantee you'll be 'satisfied', babe."

I handed her the fifty and she took my hand, this time dragging me even lower in the complex. We walked past a red velvet floor to just regular carpet. She started dancing; she pulled my cock between her ass again and bounced. She turned and sat facing me, rubbing her pussy up against my cock, and then she took herself down and slipped a hand into my pants. She tugged on my cock. I moved my hands to her pussy and gave it a stroke.

"Oi, babe. No touching. Just enjoy."

I pulled my hand away and sat there as she jerked my cock. She was rubbing the head of my cock as I came. She pulled her hand out of my pants and wiped the cum off on the carpet floor.

We walked back into the main dancing area. I looked at my watch: 3.30am. I left the club and walked back to the train station. I picked a bench on the platform and pulled some newspapers up over me, waiting for the train back home.

25

The next day, to save on money, I waited for a train to get me in past 10am. I stood on the platform and waited to board my train. There were plenty of other undesirables getting on the train with me. I was glad I wasn't alone.

I sat near the door travelling backwards. The ticket inspector came down the train. He was a fat man and he was dripping in his own sweat.

"Tickets from Sheffield. Can I see all tickets from Sheffield, please?"

I presented him with my ticket. "Is there a buffet car on this train?" I asked.

"No, pal. But there will be a cart on its way."

"Okay. Cheers."

He gave me my ticket back. I placed my head against the window and closed my eyes. When the trolley-dolly finally came, I stopped her. She charged £4.50 for a beer. But I bought one anyway.

I got off in Leeds with the tinny still in hand. I drained the can. Then I went for a run. I ran myself home: around 4-5miles. I got into the flat just gone midday. I had an hour's sleep and then I got dressed into my work uniform and headed out to the supermarket.

I made it to work on time. I clocked in and headed off to the dairy fridges. There was a note left for me.

"Grindley: Rotate meat and ready meals. Fill short life. Do deliveries."

Rotating all the stock meant that I'd have to check each individual date by eye. Then put the shortest dates to the front and the longer dates at the back.

I set out down the meat section. It took me the best part of an hour. I was dizzy at one point. My eyes couldn't focus as I was checking number after number and then lining them up in order of expiry dates.

I pulled off around twenty different sorts of meats. All expiring today. I put them out back to reduce down.

I went onto the ready meals. It took me another hour. I pulled off ten boxes of out-of-date pizzas. I took them in the back with the meat to waste them, and to reduce whatever I could to sell today. I grabbed a PDA from the desk. There were forms to fill out when taking a PDA but, since nobody was around, I just took it.

I walked back to my pile of reductions and found Rich stood over them.

"Grindley. What are you doing with all this?"

"Gonna reduce what I can. Waste the rest."

"Don't fucking waste it, you twat. These pizzas will be

fine. Just change the packaging to a pizza that's in date."

"Really? I don't want to do that."

"Do it, Grindley. Or I'll write you up."

"Okay." I sighed.

"And Grindley."

"Yeah."

"Reduce all this meat to 10p and leave it in the back for me."

He walked off with his forced, fat swagger. If one of us got caught taking home food that we'd reduced it would be a straight dismissal, but he would just take liberties.

I reduced the meat and placed it in a basket. I wrote a note on top: 'Reduced for Rich'. I hoped someone would see it and fire that fat wanker. I sat in the back and switched a load of the pizza sleeves round. We always had spares in the back with a blank spot to write in the date. The pizza sleeves would come off quite easily. I wrote the new dates in print on the front. I didn't want to give them too long out on the shop floor. I dated everything for three days' time and put it back on the shop floor as a buy-one-get-one-free offer.

I saw Deli Girl working. She smiled when I looked at her,

but she wouldn't allow herself to be caught looking my way. Each time I would watch her working, I would see the smile come across her face. She would never show a glance in my direction though. She finished before me. I saw her walking out with one of the wedge fellas that worked on the back door.

26

I skipped the next day's training. And the next. And the one after that. Coach turned up at my apartment on the Thursday morning. I met him at my door wearing nothing but a dressing gown.

"Alex. Good run at the weekend. How come you've not been back down to the track?"

"Just tired. You want a drink?" I gestured to the kettle.

"Coffee please mate."

I poured two coffees. I poured a little whiskey in mine and a sugar in his.

"Cheers Alex."

We sat and blew over the coffee. A few moments went by before he said anything again.

"I got an invite for you." He threw a letter onto the table. "To race the European Trials in Birmingham this weekend. It's a three round race and the top two will be selected to race the European indoor championships."

I picked up the letter and read it:

To whom it may concern,

We have been looking to contact Mr Grindley after he ran the qualifying mark for the European Indoor Championships. We rarely make exceptions to our entry requirement. However, given the margin that Mr Grindley has exceeded the qualification standard, we feel it would be remiss to exclude him from this excellent opportunity.

Please find timetable and other details enclosed.

Regards

Ian Van-Collins

I looked over the table at Coach.

"Do you think this is a good idea?"

"Do I think this is a good idea? Are you fucking mental? Yes, Alex. It's a fucking great idea. Fuck. You have a real chance here buddy. To do something in the sport."

"Okay."

"Okay? You'll do it?"

"Okay. Yeah. I'll race the trials."

"Good Alex. I'm glad to hear that. Do you want a lift? I can pick you up at the weekend from the supermarket?"

"Yeah, that'd be good."

27

The weekend came around fast. I waited for Coach just round from the supermarket. I hadn't even bothered to ask for the day off work, because I knew what the answer would have been. I waited out of sight. The car pulled up near and I waved from round the building. He saw my signal and drove over to me. I jumped into the car.

"Can I borrow your phone quickly? Mine's out of credit."

"Yeah sure, Alex."

He handed me the phone and I dialled in the store number.

"Hi, this is Alex on dairy. Can you put me through to the duty manager, please?"

"One moment, Alex."

"Hello, Rich speaking."

"Hi Rich, it's Alex. Are you on duty?"

"Grindley. Yeah, I'm duty Manager. What d'you want?"

"I'm ill, Rich. I won't be able to come in today."

"Ill, Grindley?"

"Yeah, Rich. You know I don't miss work. I can't afford to."

"Alright, Grindley. But if I find you're not ill, I'll fuck you hard."

He put the phone down. I handed the phone back to Coach.

"Cheers for that."

He nodded and put the phone in the door handle. It looked like it could fall loose at any point.

28

We had to park a good distance away from the venue. It was around a ten minute walk into the arena. It was hot at the track. The lights were keeping everyone warm, but people were still sat in their coats. There must have been maybe 8,000 folks there to watch the championship. I came out of the arena floor. There was a curved corridor going around the entire venue. Stalls selling food, drinks and beer were everywhere.

Coach took me down the stairs to the community sports hall. It was underneath the arena. I signed in at the desk. I gave my name and event.

"Alex Grindley, eh? I'm looking forward to seeing what you've got - it was a good run you did last week."

"Thank you."

I took my number and some pins and we made our way to the sports hall. We set up base in the far right hand corner. I started to pin my numbers onto the front of my vest.

"Right Alex. You've got three rounds. The heats shouldn't be too hard. You should be okay, but make sure you win if you can. You'll get a better lane draw for the semi's."

I finished pinning on my numbers to the back of my vest. Then I jogged around the sports hall. There was an incredibly different atmosphere to the race last week. I could feel the tension and pressure everyone was feeling. The women were a lot more toned on the whole. They didn't wear crop tops quite as casually as they seemed to last weekend.

I jogged up and down a couple of times. I sat down next to Coach and began to stretch out my limbs. I went through the motion of starting at the bottom and stretching each muscle group as I came to it. I spent around thirty minutes doing all that. I put on my spikes and did a couple of easy strides down the sports hall.

"They are calling your heat, Alex, are you ready?"

"Yep."

Coach walked me to the call room. "Good luck, Alex."

For the first time since I'd met him, he extended his hand to shake mine. I met it with a firm grip and shook it.

There was an older official signing us into the call room.

"Name?"

"Alex... Grindley."

"Okay, Alex. Heat 2, lane 4. Go and sit down in the second row."

A woman came to check my bag. She opened it up and went through it, pulling out my electronics and anything that had any branding on.

"Collect your electronics back here after the race."

I nodded. Then she began to tape over anything that was branded in my bag. She even covered the Puma logo on my bag and ripped off the labels from my water.

The other guys that were sat around me didn't say much. They were all looking down at their feet; bouncing their legs up and down nervously. I sat back and stared at them. I wanted to catch the eye of one of them to freak them out.

"Spikes on please, gentlemen."

The official pointed to our feet. A few of the guys

already had them on. I pulled my old spikes out of my bag. They were battered, worn and soft. I put them on; then joined the line to be lead out onto the track.

I set up my blocks and followed the Starter's commands. The gun went off and I pushed out of the blocks and into the race. I came down the banking for the second lap. We broke into lane one. I was in second place. I sat there just running behind him. He started to slow up badly half way round. I came out into lane 2 and ran beside him. As we hit the bend again, he had the inside lane, I couldn't quite get past. We came onto the final straight; he faded badly. I came past and took the victory.

I met Coach back in the warm up area.

"What the fuck, Alex? Just beat them to the break. Don't make yourself run wide. You won't get away with that shit in the semi-final." I could see that he was feeling the pressure more than I was.

The semi-final came along. I followed the same procedure. This time I was in lane 5. As I set up my blocks this time round, people were taking longer. When the starter called "On your marks!" I was held for a long time. I looked through my legs when I was in the crouch position; I could see that athletes were fucking around. Swaying and stretching on the start line.

The gun finally went. I had a poor start. I was focusing too much on the antics of the others. This time as I came off the curve to the break line I kicked hard. I ran past the field and straight into first place. On the second lap, I just turned my legs over. I felt one of the guys come up onto my shoulder. I increased my speed a little to keep him wide for the final corner. Then I just eased away from him.

By the time of the final, I felt exhausted. I had lane 6 in the final. When it came to "On your marks!" I took it slow. As I got into the blocks, I found a bit of plastic in my lane. I tossed it back right in front of the guy in lane 5. He was going to be the guy to beat.

This time, I came out of the blocks well. I felt like I must have gotten the quickest start out of everyone. As we went down the back straight for the first time, I could hear the guys on the inside. This time, I pushed going into the bend before the break. I worked that curve hard and came down off it clearly in front. I went through the start/finish line and the bell rang to signal that we were on the final lap. I saw the clock, it read: 20.98 through 200m - which was quick. Seeing that, I pushed for the entire second lap. I was going great. I knew there was a big gap behind me that they couldn't do anything about. As I started the final bend, no more than eighty meters out, I felt the lactic take hold of my legs. I tried desperately to keep going forward. Lowering my shoulders and trying to stay relaxed, I pumped with my arms. I could feel the guy in second coming up to me. The line finally came. I dipped and fell over. The clock stopped at 45.45. The fastest time in

Europe.

I walked off the track. There were film cameras: news crews. I walked past them. Nobody asked me for an interview. Everyone stopped the guy that finished behind me. I could hear them asking him what had gone wrong. Why had he not won? That pissed me off. I found Coach.

"We're going home."

"Already, Alex? You're the UK champion. You're probably going to be selected for the European indoor championships."

"Yeah, we're going now. I've had enough of this for the day."

We got in the car and he drove me home.

"Drop me off by this pub - if that's okay?"

"I can do. I can drop you off right at home if you want though?"

"No. The pub is fine thanks."

He pulled over and I opened the door and got out.

"I'll see you at training tomorrow?"

"Maybe."

He drove off. I walked into the pub and ordered a beer.

29

I walked into work the next day feeling totally fucked from the races. I swiped myself in on time, and made my way to see what I had to do. When I got to the board, my name wasn't down. I stood looking at it.

Rich walked by and saw me. "What are you doing here, Grindley?"

"I'm here for work. What do you want me to get on with?"

"Nothing."

"What do you mean?"

"I told you I'd fuck you Grindley."

He pulled out a newspaper. They had written about me becoming the UK champion at the weekend. There was a picture of me crossing the finish line and falling over.

"What! You can't fire me for that?"

"No, maybe not. But I can fire you for reducing meat, Grindley."

"What? I reduced that for you!"

"I wouldn't ever do that," he said it with a sly smirk across his fat face. "Get out of here, Grindley. You're fired."

I walked out and made my way across town, straight to the job shop. They knew what they were doing. Always kept you as a temp. No rights for dismissals, no severance, nothing.

I walked into the Jobcentre and signed onto the dole. It took me the best part of the day for £61 a week. I walked home. I wanted to go to the pub. But I knew I had a bottle at home. I couldn't afford the expenses now. I walked into the flat; went straight to the boiler and turned it off. Then I got the whiskey out of the cupboard and had a drink.

30

A few days later at the track, Coach had a letter for me. It was from Ian Van-Collins:

Dear Alex,

It is my pleasure to inform you that you have been selected as part of the TeamGB squad to represent at the European indoor championships in the **400m/4x400m.**

Please meet the team at London St Pancras on Thursday, no later than 12.00h.

Sincerely,

Ian Van-Collins

"That's tomorrow though. Not much notice."

"It's still great, Alex. You've got a real chance."

"Yeah, I guess. Just need to work out how to get down there."

"Just get a train."

"Trains are expensive. I might see how much the national express buses are."

"Well, as long as you get yourself to the right place, Alex."

"I will. I'm gonna go back now to pack all my crap together."

"Good luck."

"Cheers."

I walked home and began to pack a bag of kit. "Spikes, vest, tracksuit. I better put a casual shirt in. Maybe some jeans. Tooth paste an' brush." I checked items off as I put them into the bag. I walked to the cupboard and grabbed a half bottle of whiskey. I wrapped it in an old t-shirt and secured it in my bag.

I threw my bag over my shoulder and took a wander into town to the National Express offices. It was about a two mile walk. My bag, although not overly heavy, was digging into me by the time I finally got there. I looked at the advertisement boards. One-way to London: £10.

"When does the next 10 quid bus to London head off?"

"Leaves at midnight, get you to Kings Cross. St Pancras by 5am."

"That's fine, I'll get the ticket, please."

I had a solid few hours to kill. I took a stroll to an off-license and picked up a six-pack. I sat at the bus stop with my beer and waited for the bus.

It pulled up around 23.30. I got on and made my way to the back seats. I liked to secure the seats with extra legroom. I watched a few other people getting onto the bus. They all sat up near the front. Just before midnight, a fella jumped on with a guitar over his shoulder. He walked right up towards the back and sat near me. The bus pulled out.

I opened a beer and began to drink it.

"Isit a beer you got there?"

"Yeah. You want one?"

"Yeah mate."

I passed him a can and he opened it and started to drink it. He glugged it to about half way then slowed his drinking and let it sit in his hand.

"Name's Jimmy."

"Alex."

"What takes you to London Alex?"

"Catching a train to Paris."

"Well, what drags your ass to Paris?"

"Nothin' much. Heading there for an athletics meet."

"Oh yeah. I though you looked familiar. You're that Grindley bloke?"

"That's me."

"Yeah. I saw that race mate. I used to do some running."

"Really? What d'ya do?"

"I was an 800m runner. Made the final of the world indoors in 06."

"What happened?"

"Nothing. Just left the sport. Love my music." He gestured to the guitar. "That's what's taking me to London."

"Cool."

We spoke most of the way there. Jimmy had a bottle of wine in his bag. Once we'd killed the beers, we drained the wine. The bus pulled into the station just before five. I got off and said farewell to Jimmy. It was the middle of March and very cold. I was tired. I pulled some extra clothes out of my pack and put them on. I found a quiet corner out of the way and sat down. I closed my eyes and managed to doze off for a couple of hours.

When I woke, I saw a few athletes wander in wearing their GB tracksuits. I stood up and followed them. They met the Head Coach and picked up their train tickets. I walked over to the woman with the tickets.

"Can I help you?"

"Yeah. Can I grab my ticket off you?"

"Are you an athlete?"

"Yeah. Alex Grindley."

"Oh. Right. You're supposed to be in kit Alex."

"I've not got any."

"Right well, we can hopefully find you a vest to compete in. Here's your ticket, Alex. Just go and get on the train when you're ready. The whole team is in the same carriage."

I slept the whole train journey there. In Paris, we all got off the train and walked out to the front of the station. A bus picked us up and drove for around an hour to the hotel. I could see the indoor arena from the lobby. It was right next door - easy to walk to for the competition.

We picked up room keys from the desk. Each athlete had to share with someone. They had put me in with one of the high jumpers. I went up and dumped my bag on one of the beds. I sat in the chair that was in the corner of the room. My roommate put on the TV.

"Grindley, right? Nick." He pointed to himself as he said Nick. I shook his hand. He walked out of the room in his kit and went across to the arena to do a training session. I sat back and watched the TV. I grabbed my bottle out of my bag and took a couple of pulls from it. Then I wrapped it back in my shirt and put it in the bottom of my bag.

31

The competition started the next day. I was drawn in heat 4 of 5. It was the top two progressing to a semi-final, with only the winner guaranteed a good lane draw. I had realised the importance of having an outside lane when running the tight indoor bends. Especially for someone of my height. I'm 6ft 3' and those bends felt tight from the inside lanes. I was in a pretty good lane but I had the fifth fastest guy in the competition just outside me. I used him as my mark. I followed him to the break and just put in a small spurt to get past. We both ran pretty quick times. I won the heat and awaited the draw for the semi-finals.

I walked back to the hotel and grabbed some food in the dining hall. Athletes seemed to spend all day in the food hall. There were groups of familiar British athletes hanging around. I sat with them as I ate my plate of pasta. I didn't bother to engage them in any conversation. I didn't feel like it. I was nervous about my semi-final coming up that evening. I felt wrong, like an illness in my stomach that just wouldn't go. I could hardly get any food down me. I just sat and listened to the conversations. Every one of the guys would speak with a strong accent. I couldn't believe this was how they sounded. It was so strong, almost put on. Maybe it was. There was such variety in the London accent. That's what I couldn't get my head around it.

I ate what I could for lunch and then headed to my room. I laid my head down and slept. Nick was still downstairs. He seemed to only turn up in the room to sleep at night.

I woke a few hours later. It was just about time to head back to the stadium for the semi-final. I quickly jumped in the shower and then got myself dressed back into the race kit. I went for a dump before I left the room. I'd not eaten much. My shit just came out as a fucked up energy drink mess. It was worse than having the alco shits. I got downstairs in the lobby and a team manager was there.

"Hi Alex. Do you have everything that you need?"

"I got my number and my vest and my spikes."

"Excellent. I'll tick you off then. Have a good one."

She waved me off and I wandered to the stadium. It was cold outside. I didn't have a GB tracksuit top so I just went over in my vest. I jogged it to cut down the commute through the cold. I made it into the warm up area. A few of the Team Coaches were there. They were all sat in a corner looking at a TV screen, watching the athletics.

I started to warm up. I did my regular jogging and stretching. I went to do a couple of strides when I felt a twinge in my hamstring. I walked over to the Team Coaches and the therapists.

"Hey, could someone just have a quick look at my leg, please? Something doesn't feel right."

"Who are you assigned to?" one of them replied.

"Oh. I don't know."

"Well, who do you see at home?"

"No-one."

"Okay. Give me five minutes. I'll just watch this race."

I wandered to the physio beds and sat down. I must have been waiting nearly ten minutes. The therapist finally came over.

"Can you stretch it?"

"Yeah." I did a hamstring stretch to show him.

"And does that hurt?"

"No, it's okay doing this. It's when I try and bring my leg up under me when I'm running."

"I'm sure it'll be okay. Give me a shout if it gets worse."

He walked off back to the TV corner. I went to do a few more runs. I could still feel it, but I wasn't going through that shit again. I just sucked it up and walked myself into the call room. I had the former world champion in my semi. He was in the lane just inside me.

The call room felt like it lasted forever. I was just sat on a bench staring at everyone else. They were all doing the same. Occasionally, someone would jump up and move about, kicking their legs out. Doing some fast feet. I started to yawn. Repeatedly, I slapped my face with both hands in a clapping motion to try and wake myself.

Finally, we were taken out onto the track. I put my blocks in quickly. The rest of the guys took their time. I did a few practise starts. I kept looking at the clock. It was still displaying the time of day. So I knew we weren't ready to go for a while yet. I was on track for eight minutes. Finally, the cameras came on and introduced us. The cameraman came in close for my induction. I didn't like it. He invaded my space. I put my hand on the camera and pushed it back. The crowd laughed and the cameraman came in close again. This time I just turned away, so he came round chasing me. Finally, they said my name; I waved to the crowd and the cameraman finally fucked off.

I settled into my blocks and closed my eyes. The starter called "Set!" I went up and held. Then I just went. I didn't hear the gun: I just went. There was no recall gun, so I kept running. I wasn't a hundred per cent sure that I was in the race. I had a moment of hesitation. Then I heard the sound of the world champion coming up on the inside of me. We came off the curve into the break neck and neck. I gritted my teeth and moved towards the inside lane. Our shoulders came together and he pushed me off with his elbow. I bounced back onto him, this time my inside leg catching his. I stumbled a little but managed to catch myself. I came back in towards him again. I could see my leg was going to hit his once more. I held my breath and moved towards the inside lane. He put the brakes on and gave up the inside line. I lead through the break. I kicked at 200m to go - I, really dug in deep and pushed off the bend. I moved away from him down the back straight, then I heard him coming again as we came into the final stretch. The crowd were screaming. I was rocking and rolling. As he came up on my shoulder, I moved wide, pushing him wider. He kept coming up on me. I dipped at the line and I just knew I'd got it. He walked off kicking at the floor. I saw him take his spikes off and throw them into the track.

I walked off.

"Alax Grindely?"

"Alex. Yeah, that's me."

"Ah. Hallo. I am wit' anti doping. I tak' you for a drugs test now please."

"But I have a final tomorrow. Can't I go and grab some food and sleep?"

"No. I must test now."

I followed him off the track and up some stairs. He was an older man. French with grey hair and thick glasses. He wore a tattered suit with the anti-doping logo sewn onto the lapel. He sat me down in a small room. We filled in some basic forms: I had to list my name; provide some ID and give my address. Then I had to fill in any medication or supplements I'd taken in the last week.

"What classes as medication exactly?"

"Anything. It doesn't matter. Just write it down."

Just to be safe I wrote: 'Beer x 30, whiskey (bottle) x3, wine (bottle) x1, cider x 15.' I handed it back to him. He signed the bottom and gave me a copy.

I chose two bottles from a sample he gave me. After around 45 minutes of waiting, I was ready to piss. I walked to the crapper with him.

"I stand and watch."

"You what?"

"I watch you give sample."

I got my cock out and tried to piss with him watching.

"No, you must pull down pants." He gestured from nipple to knee. "I must see all this."

I pulled down my kegs and stood, bear assed, like a pissing seven year old as some old guy watched me wiz. There wasn't that much piss to come out of me.

"Little more. You need to reach this line." The old guy pointed his long finger in towards my pecker causing me to jerk away and nearly spill. I looked at the line on the bottles. I stood there a little while longer. The old guy turned on the tap. I closed my eyes and tried to relax. At last, a few extra drops came and tipped me over the line.

I pulled my pants back up and screwed the lids on the bottles. The old guy wrote down a few more things on a sheet of paper. I countersigned the bottom of it and was given another copy.

When I got back across to the hotel, dinner had finished and the restaurant was empty. I walked up to my room and got in bed. Nick was already laid in bed. He was typing messages onto his laptop. Chatting up some woman he'd probably never meet. I took my shirt containing the whiskey out of my bag and walked into the bathroom. I locked the door and turned on the shower. I sat on the toilet and drank a good quarter of the bottle. Then I wrapped it back in my shirt. Walked out of the bathroom and took myself to bed.

I lay there trying to sleep as Nick jerked off into the glow of his laptop.

32

I stood on the start line the next day for the final and I felt nothing. I had made a European Indoor final and getting there had drained my emotions. I hadn't slept well. There wasn't enough to drink. I hadn't managed to eat any food since lunch the day before and my roommate had kept me awake with his online antics.

I was slow out of the blocks, but I came into the break joint with the top three. I didn't push hard into the break this time. I let the world champion just ease in front of me, and then the other British guy bumped me down to third. I followed round the second lap, the gap was opening and then, out of nowhere, the Brit in second started to die. I pushed hard looking to beat him again. A Russian came round and passed me coming onto the home straight. I was back in fourth and out of the medals. I kept pushing trying to reclaim a position. Just meters away from the line, the Brit, the Russian and I were jostling for $2/3/4^{th}$ places. I threw myself over the line and fell to the floor.

As I lay on the floor, I looked up at the big screen,

showing the replay over and over again. Next to it the results were coming up: first place had been given to the German; second place took a while longer, then it came up: Russia. They jumped up and ran round the track celebrating. I was still awaiting the result when they were half way round their lap of honour. Finally, the result flashed up: third. I was third. An official came and pulled me off the floor by extending a hand to assist me. A flag was thrown onto the track for me and he told me to do my lap with the others. At this point, they were almost back at the finish line. I picked up the flag and put it over my shoulders. I grabbed a corner and wiped my sweat off with it.

I walked off the track without doing a lap. The TV crew tried to stop me this time to ask some questions. They weren't that interested though. I could see the guys looking out for better athletes to talk to. They didn't even notice me walk away.

When I got out to the warm up area, the relay Coach spoke to me for the first time. "Congratulations, Alex."

"Cheers."

"Come over here for a minute. I just want to talk to you about the relay." He pulled me away from a few of the other people. "Alex, man to man, I can't run you in the relay. I know you've done well, and you're in shape. But let's be honest. You ain't changed the stick with the guys; you haven't been to a single relay practice. You just don't have the skills required."

"I've not been invited to a relay practice before."

"I know, we will get you to practices and if you're still running okay by the Olympics, then I'll be in a more confident position to select you for the team. I just can't take the risk now."

Ian Van-Collins walked over to congratulate me on the medal.

"Ian. I was just telling Alex about the relay situation."

"Argh, yes. I hope you understand, Alex. We just can't run you. I hope you'll still warm up with the team?"

"Yeah. Fine."

I took myself and collected my medal. Then I sat in the hotel bar and had a few beers. I slept considerably better that night. The next day I warmed up with the relay team, but nobody spoke. They all had headphones on and did their own thing. I jogged for a while, but I was tired. The guys went in for the relay and ran. They came second. They really should have won.

33

I sat drinking in the room that night. Around midnight, Nick walked in with two black girls. They had no figures but were tight and toned and wearing tiny short skirts. One girl had frizzy hair with a lot of volume and the other had it braided long down her back.

Nick was kissing them both as he walked in; he sat down on the bed and took the top off one of the girls. She had no tits: just these nipples sitting on her chest. He undid his pants and pushed her down to his cock.

"Hey, Alex. Hope ya don't mind, pal?"

"Go for it buddy."

He kissed the other girl as he was getting sucked off. I reached out my hand and stoked the back of the girl he was kissing. She stopped kissing him and whispered something in his ear. He nodded. She came over and sat across me on the bed. I pulled off her panties and put my cock inside her.

Nick started to fuck his girl; he was stroking in from behind. I still had bottles next to my bed, so I kept drinking as I lay on my back getting screwed. Nick picked up a bottle of wine and passed it to his girl. She stopped screwing him to drink it. She got off his bed and walked onto my bed, still drinking. My girl got off me. She moved over to Nick. I put my dick in her and stoked about twenty times whilst she was drinking the wine.

Nick came round and put his cock down her throat. "Yeah, take it deep, swallow that cock," he said.

He pushed it down deep in her throat, she gagged but he didn't take it out, she moved trying to get her head away from his cock but he followed her keeping his dick pushed down her throat. She eventually got free and threw up on the floor. As she vomited, the pussy clenched hard around my cock and I came inside her.

The bottle of wine fell to the floor and she lay on the bed gathering herself. I pulled out of her and rolled her onto her front, so her head was hanging off the bed and facing the floor. She hurled again. Nick went back and screwed the other girl some more.

"You all finished up Al, or you want in?"

"I'm finished, pal."

I picked up the bottle of wine and rested my head on the buttocks of the pasted out wino. Nick went back to finish fucking and I drank, listened and then slept.

34

I got back home a few days later. I took some time off training; I had no job to go to. Once a week, I was told to go and sign in at the job shop. I had to show that I was making an effort to find work. They picked a few jobs from a list and sent off my CV to them.

At home, there was nothing to do. I couldn't afford any decent liquor, so I had value wine, value beers and value whiskey. I'd dilute all my drinks with water to make them go that little bit longer. I mainly stayed in bed, not wanting to get up. There wasn't anything to get up for. I felt strange. I just wanted to sleep, so that I might wake up well and not tired.

A couple of weeks went by with me just lounging around. Then, one morning, I received a letter inviting me on a weeklong training camp with the relay team. It was all expenses paid and I was invited to meet the team at Heathrow Airport on the Saturday.

Saturday came, and I found myself on the back seat of a National Express bus heading to the airport. I had a backpack with my running gear, spikes and a few bottles of cheap wine. The bus was filled with families all packed, going for their holidays. Women on the bus would keep looking back and either smile at me or frown; some would quickly look away if I caught them looking.

I arrived at the airport and met up with the relay team. There were only five of us. Slime, he was apparently named for his technique with the women. Jig, who was named for his success with the women. There was Spack, named for his running technique and then Terry, who just seemed to abuse everyone and get away with it. And the team was led by Coach Carl.

It was a three-hour flight to the training camp in Spain. Everyone sat out with laptops, headphones, and handheld games devices. Slime would slap me on the shoulder every once in a while and point out some woman and her arse. Maybe half of them were okay.

The other half of them were just crazily huge.

When we got to the hotel, I dropped my stuff into my room. Everyone was sharing apart from Coach Carl and myself. I had my own room. I opened the mini-bar and found that the booze had all been taken out. It was late. I went to bed and lay looking up at the ceiling.

35

I woke the next morning feeling like shit. I took a huge dump and it came out warm and soft. I could smell the shit and it made me reach deep into my stomach. I spat out a small mixture of vomit and spat in the sink.

I skipped breakfast and met the relay team at the bus stop outside of the hotel. It was only a five minute bus journey to the track. Coach Carl had hired out a bus to take us there and back every day. It was a warm enough day. We got to the track and started a workout. It was just a few easy runs and a gym session with circuits. I still felt crap. Running in the heat didn't help. After each run, I'd head into the toilets and splash some cold water over my face and body.

After the running session, we grabbed lunch. There was a small café over the road. Jig went over and brought back sandwiches for everyone. I ate them and it eased the illness slightly.

I couldn't lift the weight that the others did in the gym. I didn't know how to Olympic lift like they could. I was bigger than all of them, and I was pretty sure that I was stronger too, but I just didn't have the technique to do what they were doing. Once we got onto simples exercise like squats or bench presses, my strength came out and I felt better about myself.

We took another break before the circuits, the guys all sat around chatting. I took myself back to the toilet and threw more water over my face. I lay down until I heard Coach Carl shouting for the start of circuits.

They were the worse. I was working up a horrible sweat and feeling sick to my stomach. I gritted my teeth and pushed on through the pain. After the session was over, the guys got onto the bus.

"Grindley! Hurry the fuck up and get on the bus."

"No, Coach. I'm gonna walk it back."

Coach Carl didn't even take a second glance. He got on the bus and sat down jesting and cheering with the guys, and the bus drove off.

I got up and walked across the road to the café. I sat down outside and looked over at the track as the sun set. I ordered a couple of beers and drank quietly as a warm breeze blew against my skin.

Once the sun had set, the temperature dropped. I bought a bottle of local brandy from the guy behind the counter and set off walking home.

My room had a small balcony. I put on some music from a crappy radio in the hotel room and sat out on the deck drinking the brandy. If I sat in the far right corner of balcony, I could angle myself just right so I could see the ocean. I put my feet up on the railing, sat back and looked out as the moonlight caught the waves. I took a good hit of the brandy and began to feel a little like myself again.

36

The trip followed that pattern. After every session I'd head to the café and have a few drinks - maybe getting something to eat. The guys were very much a unit together. They spent a lot of time together back home and I don't think they liked the idea of me just walking into their team.

Towards the end of the week we got a rest day. I walked along the beach and found a nice bar; it was half on concrete and half on the sand. I sat there with a cold beer and checked out the girls walking around in bikinis and short skirts. Some of the girls were incredibly pale; I decide they had just arrived for a holiday. Some of the girls were thoroughly tanned. My favourite were the chicks that were tanned, but if you checked them out long enough you'd catch a glimpse of some white bits; as their bikini would ride up their arse or a tit would start to bounce free.

I saw the guys walking past. I gave them a courtesy

wave. They crossed over the road and started heading towards me.

"What up, Dick Balls?" said Terry.

"Not much Terry, what's up with you guys?"

"Just taking a wander out to find some bars and some chicks. Wanna come?"

"Sure thing."

I drained my beer quickly and then set off walking with the guys. Jig was checking out every chick we passed.

"Check out the arse on that one." "Look at the tits over there." "Fuck me, that bikini is riding up her snatch."

We walked along the beach that way for a good couple of miles until we found a nice little bar. We sat down for lunch. Jig was still on it: eyeballing every woman in view. "Have you seen the waitress? Fuck me. That skirt's so short you can see her snatch."

Slime raised his hand and summoned her over. "Alright darlin', can we have five beers please? Oh, an do ya have summat I can suck on?"

"What do you want to suck on, sir?"

"What do you have that I could suck on?"

"We have boiled sweets?"

"Oh yeah. I wanna suck on summat sweet."

"So five beers and a sweet?"

"That'll do for now, sweetheart."

The waitress went off and got our drinks. I was checking her arse as she walked away; it shook with real purpose as her long legs strode out towards the bar. It shook side to side violently with each footstep, but it was way too big for the rest of her body.

We drank a few rounds; the guys were all talking about things that didn't interest me. I took myself into my own world and sat and drank in their company. I zoned into the more risqué topics of conversation and, as afternoon turned to evening, there was more of it to enjoy.

"I'd love to smash that waitress! That arse is huge. I just wanna get in there an pound it," confessed Slime.

"Hahaha, you wouldn't know where to put it, Slime," replied Jig.

"Fuck you, Jig."

"Yeah. That arse is so big your dick wouldn't even reach the opening." Terry smashed the table as he insulted Slime.

"Fuck both of you. I could smash the biggest girl here and my dick would reach."

"Let's play 'Ride the Fat Bitch' then?" suggested Terry.

"Fine," they both replied.

Slime, Jig and Terry all jumped up from the table and walked off.

"Hey, Spack." I leaned in toward him. "What's 'Ride the Fat Bitch'?"

"Oh, they gotta find the fattest girl they can, you know, put in some work, and then they gotta jump on her and call her a fat bitch and see how long they can stay on her."

"Oh."

I sat back into my seat. The waitress came back over.

"You guys want any dinner?"

I turned to Spack. "You fancy summat to eat?"

"Yeah, okay."

We ordered food. I got the lasagne and Spack ordered some kind of spaghetti dish.

"And to drink?"

"Hey, Spack. You fancy a bottle of wine with dinner?"

"Oh, I don't know, should I mix drinks? You want wine do you?"

"Yeah, I might jump onto the wine."

"Well, okay then."

"Yeah, we'll get two bottles of house white, please?"

"Two bottles? I thought you wanted to share a bottle?"

"Fuck no."

I waved the waitress off, and she went with the order in hand. I checked her overly sized arse again as she strode away.

At the end of the meal, we paid the bill. I made Spack pay for all the drinks from the other guys. I gave the waitress a good tip for the arse gazing - even though it was oversized, she did wear it well.

37

We had a drink in most of the bars on the long walk back; looking to see if we could find the other guys. Spack was struggling to walk upright. He was staggering all over the street and onto the road. Near the hotel was this place with a blue neon sign outside. It had a small garden out front made from artificial grass and a live band playing inside: it was packed out. I decided that I needed another drink.

I walked towards the bar, past the dance floor where I saw Jig and Slime with two huge girls. They were dancing and grabbing the girls' arses. Slime was particularly lechery: sticking his tongue down her throat and wiping his sweat off and making her lick it. They saw us and waved like idiots. Jig went first. He jumped up on the back of his girl, and then Slime followed on the back of his own catch. They high fived and then shouted.

"You Fat Bitch! You Fat Bitch! You Fat Bitch!"

The girls tried to throw them off. Jig went down first, pulling his girl with him. She struggled on the floor trying to get out of his grip as he continued shouting at her. Seeing them on the floor, Slime raised his hands in victory and, as a result, fell straight off the back of his bronco. The big girl ran over to her friend and smacked Jig with a forearm to the back of his head. Jig let go; he stood up dazed and then received another twat to the side of his head. He went back down. Slime made his way out of the bar. I could see him stood on the side of the road out front, egging on the fight. Jig got up again, his nose was bleeding, and a crowd had now made a circle with just him and the girls inside. He swung out towards them: missing. One of the girls caught him again behind the ear. He went down and the other started kicking him. The bar men had come out into the crowd to break up the brawl. A small chap with a dark moustache dragged Jig out to the artificial grass and left him. I walked out with Spack. In all the commotion, the live band had stopped playing and I could hear, "You Fat Bitch," coming from the round the corner.

I walked round to see that Terry was nailing some fat bird down a small side street. She was laid on her back and Terry was on top with his duds round his ankles. He couldn't touch the ground; he was just throwing his head around trying to create movement as he balanced on her enormous frame.

"Yeah! You fat bitch!"

"Umm, I'm your fat bitch."

"What the fuck, Terry?" asked Slime. "What the fuck?"

"Just playing the game, fuckers! Dick reaches fine."

He turned and flipped us the bird and went back to fucking his whale.

"You fat bitch!"

38

It was just Coach Carl and myself at the track the next day. I did the workout and didn't complain that I was hung-over to fuck. My times were all down.

"Grindley, man to man, where are the others guys today? What happened last night?"

"I don't know, Coach. Just went for a walk along the beach - maybe we ate something we shouldn't."

"You made it in, Grindley."

"Yeah, but I feel a little jaded, Coach."

"I don't give a fuck, Grindley. I expect to be kept in the loop - no matter what."

"Yes, Coach."

"Good. I'm gonna go back to the hotel early. Finish up with the weights."

He jumped on the bus and it drove off. I grabbed my gear and got it all together. I headed for the café across the street and took up my seat just outside on the road. I didn't eat, but decided that a couple of beers would pull me round nicely.

I spent most of the afternoon and early evening sat nursing those beers. I took a stroll back around 8pm; as I got in sight of the hotel, I could see team bags outside next to a bus stop. I walked a little longer and saw the guys walking out: Jig with a black eye; Terry with a cut down his face and Spack with vomit stains on his shirt. Coach Carl walked out and turned to face me.

"Where the fuck have you been, Grindley!?"

"I finished the session and got a bite at the café over the road. What's going on?"

"You acting like you don't fucking know, Grindley? The boys came clean didn't they? Starting fights. Drinking. The lot of you! You, Grindley. You must not want to ever run on this squad?" He left a long pause as we stared into each other's eyes: feeling out the other. "Get your bag down here in five minutes. Trips over - we're going home."

I threw my kit into a holdall and legged it down to the lobby. We jumped onto the bus and set off for the airport. It was a long trip and nobody spoke. Slime had his headphones in listening to music. I was sat a few seats away from him and I could hear the beat. Coach Carl was only a few seats in front of me. I wondered if he could hear anything.

When we arrived at the airport, Coach Carl stood up at the front of the bus. "Because you boys have made this trip end a day early, you'll all have to pay for your own flights back."

"Coach, how much will that be?" I asked.

"About £150, Grindley - teach you not to fuck about again."

"Coach, I don't have that money."

"Well, Grindley. Looks like you'll be here until tomorrow's flight then doesn't it?"

He got off the bus and took his bag. The other guys got off and followed him to the ticket desk. I sat there and watched them all walk away. I finally got myself off the bus and walked into the departure gate. The team had gone through. I took my holdall to a corner of the building and tried to best spread out my clothes to make a bed and pillow. It was pretty late. The airport was bright and busy. I pulled a shirt over my head to try and block out the majority of the light and then I closed my eyes and tried to get some sleep.

39

Around twenty-seven hours after they had left me at the airport, I landed at Heathrow. I walked out to pick up my bus but it wasn't setting off for another six hours. I made my way to the airport bar - there was a small pub-like place hidden away. It looked the darkest and quietest corner around, so I made my way over and sat down at the bar with my holdall next to the stool and I ordered a beer. I gingerly nursed my drink so as to save some cash. I had some time to kill and I didn't want to sit in a bar and get caught not drinking - they'd throw me out like the other bums.

I'd been sat with the last quarter of my beer for around an hour when some guy came into the place. There was ample space around the bar but he decided to sit right down next to me. He sat down and looked at my drink. We didn't speak. He ordered a bottle of bud and drained it quickly. Then he ordered another.

"Do want another one there, pal?"

"You buying me a drink?"

"Yeah, why not?" He pointed to my bag: there was a

TeamGB flag on the side of it.

"Well, cheers, I'll have what you're having." He signalled the barman to get me a drink and then he turned to me and held out his hand.

"Archie Lennon, but everyone calls me Mango."

I shook his hand. "Alex Grindley."

"So tell me, Alex, what's with the flag? Some sort of sportsman?"

"Not really a sportsman, I mean, I do it, but I can't live off it."

"So what sport is it?"

"Athletics, track, sprinting."

"Yeah?" he replied. The conversation seemed dead. But I had to keep talking to him whilst I finished my beer.

"Yeah. So what is it that you do?"

"Well. I'm on the dole, but between you an' me, I can make more off my gambling than anything else. I don't even like to call it gambling to be honest. It's not gambling so much when I play. My money is safer than any of those stock market guys."

"How do you work that?"

"Okay, when I play roulette, I play the numbers on the

wheel. If you know the dealer, you know how his roll works; you can predict the number to within five or six places. All you gotta do is know the wheel."

"You'll have to explain this to me. I don't see how you can get the win - you're saying the dealer is in on it?"

"No, no, if the dealer releases at 00, and I've seen it rolls seven times before landing, and the wheel turns eight times in that spin, then I'd bet a group of numbers like: 2, 14, 35, 23 and 4 - because they are all next to each other."

"And this works?"

"Yeah, sometimes I might drink a little too much and my predictions go off, but for the most part it's fine."

We went back to our drinks. Occasionally, he would tell me a few of his gambling stories: how he was banned from certain casinos for winning too much money. He said it didn't matter anyway; he was getting more into sports betting and going to the races. I told him a few of my stories - just the funny bits. We spoke about women. He told me how his long-term girlfriend had gotten fat after their second kid, and now she was just trying to drain him for child support payments.

By the time I left for my bus, I'd got a good buzz on. I took the back seat and lay across it. I used my bag as a pillow and I slept all the way back to Leeds.

40

A couple of days after I'd got back; I was in the Jobcentre, trying to get my dole payments. I had a list of places written down that I'd tried to get work at - they were all bars. I just asked when I was sitting down if there was anything going - I didn't really want the answer to be yes. I sat down with one of the advisors.

"Ah, Mr Grindley. Where were you last week?"

"I was with TeamGB on a relay training week."

"Right, well, you didn't come in Mr Grindley, so it makes it difficult for us to put you through the system to receive funds."

"I couldn't come in. I told you I was away."

"You could have gone to the Jobcentre wherever you were."

"I was in Spain."

"Really? Well, that does cause us some issues, Mr Grindley. Were you not aware that in leaving the UK you have forfeited your rights to unemployment benefits?"

"I think the fact I'm sat here now proves that I was not aware of that."

"Well, I am sorry Mr Grindley, there is nothing I can do.

You are no longer entitled to benefits. If you are still unemployed in eight weeks we can reregister you again - providing you have no more absences in that time. You will still be required to come here each week to be eligible."

I said nothing; I just took a long hard look at him; sat back in the chair and took a deep breath. Then I got up and walked out of the Jobcentre. I made my way back to the supermarket and asked at the information desk for an application pack. I filled it in there and then and handed it back to the girl behind the counter.

41

It was just over a week before I heard back from the supermarket. One of the female managers called me up: Lauren she was called.

"Alex Grindley?"

"Yeah."

"Hello, its Lauren from the supermarket. I'm calling about your application."

"Umm."

"Can you come in this evening for an interview and a work trial?"

"Yeah, that's fine. What sort of time?"

"Can you make 6?"

"Yes, no problem."

"Great, I'll see you then."

The phone line went dead. It had just gone three in the afternoon. I routed through my clothes to find the smartest gear I could, then I started walking to the supermarket - stopping for a couple of pints on my way there.

I arrived just before six; Lauren met me at the information desk. She was a moderately attractive lady, early 40's maybe. She wore a tight pair of trousers and her bum just pushed out of them. I let her lead the way to the interview room; as she walked, I watched her arse move and bounce with each step.

We sat down in the interview room and I answered all the questions as best I could. I tried to hide my disdain for the job that I already knew I hated; I tried to come across as positive and as optimistic as possible.

"Right, Alex, this all seems good. Are you alright to go and do a work trial now?"

"Work trial?"

"Yes, just do, say, a five hour shift now and we'll see how you get on."

She pointed me out to the department: it was for an

electrical job. I was standing round; keeping the stock tidy on the shop floor; taking count of the inventory in the back. I had to put security tags on all the electronics and just generally help people. It was significantly easier work then what I'd done before, but just as boring.

At the end of the shift, Lauren was chatting to one of the managers on the other departments. I kept looking over to try and see if she was going to come over to me. I tried to look busy. She finally finished her conversation and walked over.

"Right, Alex. I'm pleased with what you've done tonight, but I'm not sure if you're the right fit for this department. I think we could find something more suited to you."

"Right, like what?"

"Well, I was just chatting to Steve, and he has space for you to do a work trial on Saturday 14.00-midnight - if you can make that?"

"Yeah, I can do that."

"Alright great, Alex. Steve will meet you at the information desk on Saturday then."

42

On the Saturday morning, I was at the track like most days. The weather had started to improve and I was going reasonably well. I'd received a lot more attention since the indoor medal. At the end of the workout, Coach came over.

"Alex. Next Saturday there is a small Grand Prix in Germany and I had an email the other day asking if you'd race there?"

"Oh, I'm not sure, unemployment tells me if I leave the country I don't qualify for payments and I'm a little short on cash anyway."

"No, Alex, they will pay for your travel, and there is prize money: two sections race against each other and the top three fastest times take home £500, £300 and £100 - depending on placing."

"You think I can make a top three?"

"Yeah, you're running well, Alex. Take a chance."

"Okay, I'll do it."

Coach organised with the German counterparts all the details and logistics of the event and travelling to it. I just got told where to pick up the taxi; what flight to get and what flight to get back home again.

43

That afternoon, I met Steve for the work trial. I was on home supplies, little knick-knacks and so on: mops, bins, car oil, ironing boards - all sorts of crap. I worked alone the entire evening as Steve stayed in the canteen watching Saturday night TV.

There wasn't much to do really. I just kept getting asked questions on home improvements, or where various things where, but the customer could never name the product; they always vaguely described it.

I had to put out some stock. It was all on crates without wheels. I walked about the back to find a jack of some sorts. I wedged it under the crate and managed to lift most of it around two inches off the ground. I'd push it and get maybe around six feet before it'd drop back down to the ground. So I repeated the actions over and over; each time I'd fight to get it moving and as it fell, stopping suddenly, it would jerk me to an immediate halt, wrenching my joints about their sockets. I continually repeated this biblical punishment until I'd finally made it to the location on the shop floor.

Around 10pm, there was a call out specifically for me to go to the checkouts. I walked down and met one of the team leaders who was patrolling the tills.

"Alex, hi. I know you were checkout trained when you worked here before, so just jump on number 12 for us will ya?" He pointed to the checkout and went straight back to his patrol line. I sat on my checkout mindlessly scanning.

I started rating each woman who came to my till. I didn't just rate them on their looks, but took into account their clothing, curves; even what they had bought. One woman came through with a bottle of vodka and a bottle of coke. I didn't think much to her drink choice, but she was young. Steve finally came down at midnight; he started speaking loudly to me even as he was approaching.

"Alex, great job tonight, pal. I just don't think I have the hours to offer you though. Maybe you can do a work trial on checkouts?" He waved over the team leader who approached and entered our conversation.

"I was just saying, Luke, that Alex could do a work trial on checkouts for you guys?"

"Yeah, we can take him. Can you do five till ten Monday to Friday next week?"

"A five day work trial? That seems a bit much doesn't it?"

Steve excused himself and walked off.

"I know it seems like that, but we need to get a feel for your scan times and idle times, so we need you in over a five day trial - we do it with all of our applicants."

"Well, alright then, but can I check that you actually have the hours to offer me after the trial?"

"I'm sure we will do, Alex, providing you're right for the checkouts."

44

I took an easier week at training: I wanted to feel as fresh as possible for the race at the weekend. A chance to win money had really motivated me. Right now, I was working for free at the supermarket and training for free at the track - I felt like I was the world's biggest lackey.

I worked every shift at the supermarket that week. I continued to check out the girls. When they had men with them, I'd look to see if I would have picked the match; in some cases I would have never put them together. I looked at those girls and I knew what they were thinking: draining some poor sap dry and moving onto the next guy. Some chicks just couldn't be alone; some just cut through men taking all they could and coming out clean and fast on the other side. For the most parts, it was the guys in a nice sports coat with decent car keys that got the top girls.

I scanned repetitively all week, asking the same questions to each customer. I actually preferred those that didn't try and engage me; as a general rule the less eye contact the better. Nothing was worse than a happy, over-zealous customer. They'd never ask how you were, but told you their life stories in the few minutes you spent scanning their shopping. On Friday, the store was quiet and I just sat at my till and looked mindlessly at the clock. Friday night was finally finished and, on cue, Luke came over.

"Alex, pal. I'm sorry, I tried to say that you'd do all right on the checkouts, but it isn't going to happen, I'm afraid, pal. I have managed to sort you out with a gig on produce though."

"Really? When I am supposed to do a work trial on produce then?"

"They need you in next Wednesday and Thursday, two till midnight shifts."

"Fine."

45

I walked out of there and went over the road to the pub. I had a couple of swift drinks there then took a bottle of wine back home. I packed my gear for the weekend, drank half the bottle and caught a couple of hours' sleep before a taxi turned up for me on the Saturday morning.

He took me to the airport: it was a 7am flight. The driver was a short, Asian man. I kept seeing his eyes look at me in the rear view mirror. I finished the wine in the taxi on the way there. When we got to the airport, the driver opened the door for me then held out his hand for a tip: I gave him my empty wine bottle and walked into the terminal building.

I didn't drink on the flight - even though it was free - instead I just ate a few packets of the nuts and crisps they gave out. It wasn't a long flight; we were only in the air for just under an hour. I sat near the front, where the stewardess' were for take-off and landing. Their uniform was a tight pencil skirt. As they sat down for the landing sequence, I kept trying to get an angle to see as much up the skirt of one of the girls as possible. She kept looking back at me and moving her legs away from my line of sight. As I exited the plane in Germany, I gave her a wink at the door.

We landed in a small airport. I walked out right onto the runway and there was a man holding up a card with my name on it. I walked over and confirmed that I was Alex Grindley by showing him my passport. He signed a form and put it in his top pocket, and then he hurried me into a car saying something in German that I didn't understand. As we drove off, I saw other passengers been escorted into a small terminal building.

He drove fast. I couldn't really see much of the surroundings; it was just road and trees, until we finally came to a town after forty-five minutes. The buildings looked nice; it all looked very similar. The architecture was definitely what I'd describe as 'German'.

We arrived at the hotel. The man ushered me out quickly and carried my bag up to what was to be my room. He gestured to me that I needed to get my kit bag ready and get off to the track. I pulled a few things out and followed him back to the car. He took off again and dropped me five minutes down the road at an athletics track with a small stadium. I got out of the car, and then he pointed me in a direction and shoed me off that way with his hands.

I walked a little way and then found a desk with an English-speaking woman and a list of names. She knew me instantly.

"Alex Grindley? Yes you are. I recognize you from the European Indoors."

"Yes, thank you."

"Here is your number. You are in the race in two hours and you can warm up inside the stadium."

She pointed me on my way and I disappeared from her view as I wandered under the grandstand to make my pre-race preparations.

46

A German 400m runner had waited whilst I raced; as I crossed the finish line she gave me a hug. I had spoken to her a little before. She had not run well. I had done pretty well. I'd won my section and come second overall. She walked me to the podium. I stood up and received applause from the crowd along with a single rose and two bottles of German wine.

We walked back to the hotel. By the time we got there, we'd drunk the first bottle of wine. I had given her my rose and she had fashioned it into her hair. She had dark hair and light freckles on her face. She had a pierced belly button and was slim with small breasts. She wore very little and had a great arse. I arranged to meet her for dinner that night.

I went to my room and took a long, cool shower. I opened the second bottle of wine and took long pulls on it as I got myself into some decent eveningwear. I hadn't brought much with me. Just a checked red and white shirt and an old pair of denim shorts.

I got downstairs and she was sat waiting for me, wearing a tight, white dress. It was short - it reminded me of a tennis dress. I handed her the remainder of the wine and she threw it back and gulped the last of it. We walked into the bar. I ordered a whiskey and she had a vodka and coke.

It was a nice bar. Nicer than most I'd been in. It had a dark wood floor. The bar itself was black and decorated with red towels and coasters. The windows were covered with a rich, red curtain and a soft, black netting over that. They had a good selection of music playing. Soft rock. I liked it. I ordered another whiskey.

Her English wasn't great, and my German was basically non-existent. I had picked up a few phrases. I knew how to order drinks in most languages. I could curse somewhat and drop a few nouns into the conversation. We sat drinking for around a half hour. She impressed me; she wasn't letting me get more than a drink ahead of her.

The music changed to a more vibrant beat. She necked what was left of her drink and started dancing. She moved about and I watched her: the way her hips moved and circulated. Her hands were waving about the place and she dragged them over her body. She extended them towards me; I reached out and touched them. She clasped at me and dragged me up off my stool. I moved awkwardly to the music. I wasn't much of a dancer.

I stood writhing to the music for a while. I was mostly just staring at her and enjoying her as she grinded up on me. My cock started to get hard; I was stood there with a semi as she rubbed herself against me in time to the music. I made a hand signal at her that I was going to get another drink. I moved to the bar and ordered another couple. One for me and another for her. She kept dancing, her eyes would look about the room, and they kept coming my way. She would make eye contact then instantly look down at the floor. She always smiled when she saw me looking at her. I drank my drink; she still hadn't come over, so I drank hers too.

I walked over to her and moved awkwardly to the music again; then I leaned in close to her ear. "Do you want to come up to my room? I'll get us a bottle and we can head up?"

"I no really understand."

"Shall we go and fuck?"

"Errrr... I understand no."

I thought about giving a demonstration of my index finger screwing a hole of a clenched fist, but I reconsidered.

"That's okay."

I smiled and then turned to go to the bar. She grabbed my hand as I turned and said something to me in German.

"What are you saying?"

She pulled me close and kissed me. Our lips pushed together; I opened my mouth and lightly pushed my tongue out to meet hers. We stood kissing on the dance floor. Still holding my hand, she began to walk to the elevators. We got there and pushed the button. The lift eventually came. We walked inside and she selected floor five. The doors closed and we went back to kissing. I dropped my hand onto her thigh and felt her warm skin. I dragged it up, pulling up her dress with me. We fell out of the lift all over each other. I followed her to her room and she kept giggling as I had refused to take my hands off her soft, warm, sexy skin.

We got onto the bed. She lay down. I undid my belt and took my shorts off. Then I lifted her dress. She had a tiny G-string on. I pulled it to one side and went down on her. She had a freshly trimmed cunt. I rolled my tongue over her clit. She grabbed my head and pushed me harder onto her pussy. She put her head back and was throwing out German profanities; I recognized a few. I fought against her grip on my head and came up for air. She looked at me and said something softly to me that I didn't understand. I came up and kissed her. Then I slid my cock into her and stroked a few times. She was moving underneath me. I hooked up one of her legs and hit it again, and then I hooked up the other leg. I noticed a tattoo on the bottom of her back. It was right above the top of her arse. I pounded into her a few more times. She seemed to like it. She grabbed her ankles and pulled her legs right back behind her head. I took a firm grip on her waist and dominated her. I smashed her as hard as I could. She didn't weigh much; I was able to almost hold her in mid-air as I relentlessly rammed in my cock.

She shouted more in German. I took it as a good sign. I started to get the feeling; I rubbed inside her a few more times and then came. I pulled out and wiped myself off on her white dress. It left a cream stain.

She got up and headed to the bathroom to wash herself down. As soon as she had closed the bathroom door, I opened the mini bar. I grabbed a couple of miniatures. I opened one of them, and put the others in my pocket. I walked quietly past the bathroom and opened the door into the hallway.

I'd drunk the small bottle by the time I reached the elevator. I dropped it into a plant pot that was sitting next to the lift. I got in the lift. Pushed the button for my floor. It closed and I leant back against the wall. I reached in my pocket and pulled out another miniature and drank that. Then I headed to my room. I sat back on the bed, with the German speaking TV quietly on in the background. I drank the rest of the miniatures and fell asleep.

47

A week went by and I hadn't heard anything back from the supermarket, probably because I'd called in to say I wouldn't do another work trial unless there was a job waiting for me.

I'd got a couple of hundred quid from the race at the weekend so I had paid my rent up till the end of the month and I'd stocked my fridge with some food and a few bottles of branded whiskey. I'd even put some fuel in my car. The battery wasn't too good anymore, since it hadn't been driven in nearly half a year. I had to get it jump-started the first time, and after that I always had to do a push start to get her going.

I was sat on my front door step on the Saturday afternoon with a bottle of whiskey. I was soaking up the warmth from the sun and watching people in the street. There was a homeless shelter not too far away; I could see the bums walk off to their begging spots in the morning and then head back in the evenings. I was watching the street to see when the first few would start heading back. I saw Coach pull round the corner in his car and head for the flat. He pulled up outside and got out.

"Hey, Alex."

"Coach."

"Got you another race."

"Yeah? How's the money?"

"There isn't any this time Alex, but they will pay for your travel and give you some food money when you're there."

"I really need the money, Coach. I don't think I should go and race for free."

"I know, Alex, but you need to think big picture. You've really not got much time if you seriously want to qualify for the Olympics. You do want that right?"

"Of course I do, but what's the point of been an Olympian if I'm homeless?"

"C'mon, Alex, if you're an Olympian then good things will happen to you. Just follow your dreams and the money will come."

"I don't know, maybe I'll just hold out for something

that does pay."

"Alex. Let me be frank with you. You're not running this weekend, I have you this race in Italy next weekend which is the last chance to qualify for the European Championships and the Europeans are the last chance to qualify for the Olympics, if you don't race next week, you will not make the team. People aren't phoning me to get you races - it's very much the other way round."

"Alright."

"Alright you'll do it?"

"Alright I'll think about it."

Coach got back into his car and drove off. I poured myself another glass of whiskey and looked up. I saw him go around the corner and out of sight. I sat there until the bums started to walk back home. Then I got in my car and put the key in the ignition; with one hand on the wheel and the door open I started to push until I had enough speed to turn the key. The engine struggled, but started, and then I jumped in and drove off, heading to the casino.

When I got to the casino, I drove around for a while. I headed a couple of streets past trying to find a hill to park on. I found one not five minutes away, so I drove up it and left my car parked facing downhill - I would need the roll to get her started up again.

It was nice inside the casino: warm and quiet. Not too many tables were playing. I changed all my cash for chips and sat at the bar a while. I ordered a beer and drank it while the tables warmed up. I went over to the roulette and looked at the numbers, trying to see the groupings. The dealer released the ball. I landed my bet on 5. It wasn't even close. I did the same thing again and dropped a bet on 22 and again I just wasn't close. Next time, I bet on black and won at 2-1 so I bet black again and it came up red. I did this a couple more times and was about breaking even. I ordered another beer and just stood back and watched the table.

I worked out a system - that's all gambling is, well good gambling - working out your system and sticking to your rules. If you don't keep to your rules that's when you lose.

I walked up to the table again and put five on black. It was red, so I put ten on black. It was red again. This time I put fifteen on black, and it was black, so I took thirty back and I was even again. This was a sure fire way to stay even and, if it was your night, then you could take it and have a good run. All you needed was enough money to keep doubling your bets.

I ordered another beer to the table and kept my system going. I wasn't going up too much, but I wasn't losing money either. I had a couple more beers whilst I was playing. A few hours went by and I summoned the waitress over again.

"Another beer, please."

"I'm sorry, sir, you've reached your tab limit."

"What?"

"Yes, sir, we don't let non-members owe the bar more than £50 at any one time, unless it's been cleared by management."

I looked down and counted up my chips. I had just fifty-five pounds in chips and no other cash. I gave her the lot and walked away from the table.

"Sir, do you want another beer?"

"No."

She held out a five-pound chip back to me.

"You keep it darlin', your arse earns you a decent tip."

I walked back to the car on the hill. I sat in and took the brake off to let her roll down a little; then I turned the key, she slowed up on me as she struggled to started.

"C'mon, c'mon!"

I was nearly at the bottom of the hill but she wouldn't start up. I pushed her to the side of the road and started to walk back home. I walked at least five miles back in the cold of night. When I arrived at the flat, Coach had pushed a letter under my door with my travel details for the race in Italy with a note saying: 'None refundable'.

48

I went to the race in Italy. The meeting organizer met me at the airport. She was gorgeous. A tall brunette, short hair and she wore a small, black and yellow dress that she filled well. She had big breasts that were trying to escape the dress and a fantastic arse that gave her an hourglass figure.

The race went well. I won the event by a decent margin and gained the qualifying time for the European's.

I shared a room with this sprinter. He was a laugh. After the race, we sat and drank together. His name was Frank. He was a hurdler, I think from the U.S. - judging by the accent.

We went down to the hotel bar and picked up a couple athletes. We took a few bottles of local wine and found a sofa near one of the stairwells in the hotel. We sat there and drank, talking shit the whole time. There was this young hurdler; she was from the Mediterranean somewhere. She had an exotic name. She had darker tanned skin with dark hair down to the shoulder. Her top was tight, she didn't have much of a figure up top: a flat chest and toned arms with the slight sign of a 6-pack coming through. Her legs were long and smooth. She had the greatest arse of everyone that was around.

We ran out of booze so I went to get a few more bottles. The meeting organiser was sat at the bar so I pulled up a stool next to her.

"Chau, Alex."

"Hi."

"Well done today. You were good."

"Thank you. It was a good race, a good meeting even."

"Was it? Oh good. I'm glad you thought so."

"Didn't you think so?"

"I don't know. Errr. I just run around panicking all day and hoping."

I smiled at her. She was nursing a near empty glass of whiskey; her fingertips just stroking at the rim.

"Do you want another drink?"

"Oh, I'm not sure."

"Well, I am."

I ordered two whiskeys. The bar man came and I gave him my room number. He charged the room and poured us a healthy portion. I grasped my drink firmly and held it tight for as long as there was liquor in it. She brushed her fingertips around the glass again and played with the drink.

We got another couple of rounds in. The whole time, I kept looking her up and down. I was watching her legs in that short dress. As she drank she became less ridged and let her legs open slightly more. I could see she was wearing little, black, frilly panties.

We got another round of drinks in. The barman left the bottle just tucked under the bar in front of us.

"Charge this round to my room," she said. She looked at me intensely and placed her hand on my leg. "Room 606." She picked up the freshly poured drink and threw it back. "I'll meet you up there."

I watched her walk off to the elevator, my eyes fixated on that fantastic Italian arse, perfectly curved. I necked my drink. The barman took the glasses and walked round the bar. When his back was turned, I jumped up and reached over, grabbing what was left of the bottle. Then I turned and made my way to the lift and punched in floor 6.

I knocked on room 606 and she opened the door, dressed in just a bra and panties. I walked in and kissed her, pushing the door closed as I crossed the threshold. We fell onto the bed. I took off my top as she ferociously clawed at my belt and jeans. I kissed her neck and she put her hands on my head, she pushed me down her body. I let her move me and I kissed her all the way down, my hands caressing her legs and groping at her arse.

She pushed my head down to her pussy. I took hold of her panties and pulled them firmly to one side. She had a full muff sitting on top of her vagina, but it was nicely trimmed round the lips. I pushed out my tongue and felt the warm taste of her soft wet clit. I worked around that area, lightly circling my tongue round, and then I took two fingers and slid them inside of her. As I pushed them in, I could feel the light contours and ridges inside of her. She moaned and then pushed my head down hard into her cunt. I responded by firming up my tongue. She started to thrust her pussy forward into me; her slit was riding all over my face. I pulled away so my face could recover from the hard fucking.

I pulled my cock out of my pants and turned her over onto all fours. I pushed inside of her. Her panties were still pulled to one side. As I stroked a few times, I felt her come - she became so wet and loose. I pulled out and rubbed my hand over her pussy. I put my cock back inside her; then with the pussy juices, I rubbed her arsehole and then slid my thumb in side her ass. Her pussy became tighter; I stroked in a few more times and came.

She rolled onto her back. A light shimmering of sweat had covered her body. She was panting.

"Wow. That was good." Then she turned to look at me. "Do you want to clean up?" She pointed to the bathroom.

"Yeah, thanks."

I turned on the tap over the sink and splashed some water over my face to take off the vagina residue. I dangled my cock over the basin and threw a splash of water over it for good measure. I left the bathroom and then kissed her goodnight and walked out back into the hallway.

I got half-way to my room when I realised that I'd left the bottle in her's. I didn't want to knock on again though, so I walked to the lift and got in to go to the bar. As the doors opened at the bottom, my Mediterranean Princess was there.

"I have been looking for you. Where are you going?"

"Oh, I just felt off it. I'm heading to the bar."

"Bars just closed. You fancy a walk?"

"Yeah, okay."

She took my hand and pulled me outside. I passed Frank at the entrance as he was walking back in. We walked out and round the hotel, then back in through the doors, neither of us said anything, but she held onto my hand the entire time. We got back into the lift and she turned to me.

"Frank has a pencil dick."

"Too bad for Frank."

"Do you have a big cock?"

"I'd have to let you decide that."

She hit the emergency stop on the elevator and unzipped my fly; she pulled out my cock and played with it until it became hard.

"That's a big cock."

"Oh good."

She put it in her mouth and bobbed back and forth whilst working the shaft with her hand, she came up for air, still lightly twisting the shaft.

"Oh yeah, it's nice and thick."

The lift started to move again; she jumped up as I quickly tried to tuck my pride back into my jeans. I couldn't, and the lift doors opened with me fumbling my cock back into my pants. We walked out of the lift. I didn't make eye contact with the woman who walked in. I just ignored the fact my cock was flag-polling through my fly.

We went into a storage room off the corridor. I pulled my pants down to my knees and sat on the floor. She took her bottoms off and sat on me, rubbing my cock against her pussy.

"You don't have anything do you? You know... STDs?"

"No. Do you?"

"No."

She put my cock inside of her and started to bounce on it. She had a tight cunt; I could feel every movement intensely. I tried to move to turn her over onto her back; she wrestled me back down and held the top spot.

"Don't come inside me."

"Okay."

She kept working my cock, riding up and down; she came right up so just the tip was hanging on and took the whole shaft deep into her. I just lay motionless as she kept moaning and thrusting.

"Say my name."

I was taken by shock.

"Errr…"

"Say my name."

I couldn't remember her name - it was strange and exotic.

"Say my fucking name."

"Mediterranean Princess. My Mediterranean Princess."

"Don't you fucking cum inside me."

"Okay, okay."

I started to climax as she said it, it was feeling good, and I didn't want to pull out now, so I stayed quiet.

"Are you going to cum? Don't you fucking cum inside me you dick. You are aren't you? Don't you fucking cum."

She pulled off me and slapped my cock hard, and then put it back inside of her. It ached deep in my stomach. She went a little while longer. I started to get the feeling back in my cock. Then I felt her cream on my dick and she pulled off.

"What about me?"

"I would have finished you off, but you were going to cum in me."

"No I wasn't, you just slapped my cock, you crazy bitch."

"Well if you wanna cum, then go finish yourself off."

She smiled as she said it; she took intense pleasure from having the upper hand over me.

I pulled up my pants and went to walk out of the door. She grabbed me and kissed me passionately and then walked out in front of me. I followed her out with my pants still at knee height. Frank and a few others were stood in the hall and caught me with my pants down. I quickly pulled everything up and tucked myself away. My Mediterranean Princess just walked herself down the hall without looking back.

I got up the next morning and jumped in one of the later buses to the airport. The meeting organiser was sat at the front with the driver. We arrived at the airport and she said her goodbyes to everyone and thanked them for a good meeting, as they in turn thanked her. I was at the back of the bus and got off last.

"Thanks for everything," I said to her. "I'll hopefully see you next year?"

"I don't think so, Mr Grindley. I don't think this is a good place for you to come back to."

"Oh, okay."

I walked into the airport as she got back into the bus and drove away. About a half hour later, I got a call on my phone coming through: it was the meeting organiser.

"Hello."

"Alex, I'm sorry about before, but I need to ask."

"Ask what?"

"Well, they were talking about you and laughing about last night."

"Oh, what do you want to ask?"

"Did you screw that girl?"

"Which girl?"

"The hurdler."

"I'm not sure exactly who you're talking about."

"The tanned girl with dark hair. There were only three girls that stayed last night.

"Oh, I know who you mean, errrr… no. I think I saw Frank with her at some point. I just went back to the room."

"Oh. Good. Okay then, I'm sorry about before."

"That's fine, don't worry about it."

"Of course, I'd love you to come back next year, and maybe come and visit again soon?"

"Yeah, maybe."

We hung up. I boarded my flight and turned my phone off. I made the most of the free bar on the flight. When we landed, I turned my phone back on and it beeped with new massage. It was from the organiser again:

"Don't ever come back."

I deleted it and walked off the plane.

49

I got a letter through the post on my first day back home from Ian Van-Collins. It was congratulating me on achieving the European standard and notifying me of my selection to the team which was leaving on the Wednesday, in just 2 days' time. I was to wear my kit from the Indoor's as there was to be no more made available to me. There was an additional note at the bottom informing me that this was the last chance to qualify for the Olympic Games; with the Olympic team set to be announced the day after the European Championships.

I opened my fridge and made myself a sandwich and grabbed a beer to wash it all down with.

I headed out to the track for an evening session with Coach.

When I got there it was dark. Coach was stood waiting for me and held out his hand to congratulate me.

"Alex, mate. Well done. You've basically done all that you need to. Just go to these champs and have a good set of runs - there's nothing more we can do."

"What about training tonight?"

"Don't worry about it, buddy, I just want you to jog a few laps and we'll do some stretches. You've got a whole load of racing coming up."

I did the light workout with Coach and then he dropped me off at home. I got my gear together that night and the next day I set off to meet the team and travel to Finland for the European's.

50

The night before my first round, Ian Van-Collins gave a speech to the team and I sat there listening to it, telling me how my life was to be at the Olympics and what it would mean to me to win medals. He told me I would be happy if I could only succeed. I walked out of the meeting and straight to the bar. 'That sort of emotional bullshit might work on the masses', I thought to myself, 'but not me'.

The next morning a team manager was banging on my door. "Grindley! Grindley, get the fuck up!"

"Yeah, I'm up, what the fuck are you doing?"

"You have to be in call in an hour - get the fuck downstairs and on the bus to the track."

"Yeah, don't worry I'm ready."

My head was pounding and I was still laid in bed. I looked on my bedside table and saw a small amount of whiskey left. I drank it and immediately started to feel better. I threw on my kit and went down and got on the bus.

I did a real quick warm up and was ushered to the call

room. I sat down and began to feel sick. I was sobering up again and my head was starting to hurt. On top of that, I hadn't eaten for a good while and now and I was hungry and I felt like shit. There was nothing I could do at this point.

On track, I set up my blocks and took a drink of water, but it didn't help much. When the gun went, I came out of my blocks as easily as I could. I took it real easy down the back stretch and at the half way point I took a look at where I was. I wasn't last. I was maybe fifth of sixth. I ran the next curve a little harder. People started to fade around me and I came off in third place. Running down the home straight, I just decided to relax knowing the top three would go through. My head was pounding so I closed my eyes and just kept going. I opened my eyes at three-second intervals, just to check where the finish line was. The last time I opened my eyes, I noticed the clock had stopped, so I must have passed the finish line. I looked up at the big screen and to my surprise saw that I had won the race.

I headed back to the hotel and ate as much food as I could until I felt like bursting. I made my way back to my room and tried to sleep off my first round hangover.

Two days later, after successfully navigating the semi-finals, I was in the final and in the outside lane. I couldn't see what the rest of the field were doing until the home straight. This time, I closed my eyes to try and deal with the pain in my legs from fatigue. When I opened my eyes at intervals, people just seemed to be pulling away from me. I had a real tussle with a French guy just inside me, his arm kept striking mine the whole way down the straight; try as I might, I just couldn't move past him. I crossed the line in fifth place: 0.09 seconds away from third and 0.15 away from the winner.

I walked off the track and through the media zone. I refused to stop for anyone except this one chick who was wearing the shortest skirt and far too much makeup.

"Alex, how was the race for you? Are you happy with it?"

"I'm happy with it if you'll come out for a drink with me tonight?"

"Errr... Alex, do you think you have done enough to make the Olympic team?"

"If I had, could I see what's under that skirt?"

She stopped the camera from filming. "Alex, can you please answer the questions properly?"

"If I can see you for a drink later I will."

"I didn't think athletes drank?"

"Shit! What sort of a life is that?"

"A professional one."

Then she walked away from me, so I continued walking myself back to the bus and then back to my hotel. It was a long walk, so I stopped into a bar on the way back, still in my track kit. The man behind the bar pointed me out.

"You have just run?"

"Yeah, I've just run."

"How did you do?"

"Why don't you buy me a drink and I'll tell you all about it?"

I pulled up a stool at the bar and he put a pitcher of beer in front of me. The bar was quiet - just a few old drunks. I sat down and they all came over and lent in to hear the story.

51

The phone calls were coming in thick and fast. The European champs were over. It was a mixed bag for me. The press had taken their own interpretation of what I was feeling. How I was doing. They claimed to know my aims and ambitions. They called me whilst I was traveling back. I picked up the first few calls.

"Alex?"

"Yes."

"Can we just have a few moments to talk with you?"

"Can you call me tomorrow?"

I took a few more calls like this. One of the reporters wouldn't stop. He kept asking questions, trying to pull a quote. I wasn't budging.

The Olympic team was to be announced in 24 hours. They could all just wait. None of them gave a fuck before. I didn't want to concern myself with them. I was starting to believe that they just couldn't put me down. One thing you realise when you've got nothing is you do what you need to do to stay alive: those tasks that the middle classes see as just too hard. I could always do them. Otherwise, I just wouldn't be alive, they liked that about me I guess.

I stopped answering calls. I wasn't replying to messages. I got on my flight and sat down with a whiskey. They brought out sandwiches. "Coronation chicken or soft cheese?" I had the chicken. I watched a soft-core porno with a mediocre story. I tried to keep my screen hidden, but I knew everyone was looking at me. I could feel the disapproval. I had a semi and watched the entire movie. All one hundred minutes of it, and nobody said a word.

I sat near a girl in tiny shorts. She had great legs. A little chunky, but smooth. The middle seat was vacant between us. Once my porno had finished, I got a small bottle of red wine and sat back and looked at her legs. I didn't want to look at her face - I didn't want her to see me looking. But it felt right for me to just stare at those fine legs.

52

I got the call from Coach Carl.

"Grindley, we're going to take you as a relay runner for the Olympics."

"Relay runner?"

"Yeah, you were just short of what we expected for the individual."

"But I ran the time?"

"You ran the Olympic standard yes, but we set our own standards, and you didn't make that. You're still coming out with the relay team. You should be proud of yourself."

"Right, yeah, thanks."

"We have released the list of team members to the press this morning and no doubt you'll get some phone calls, if you've not already."

I hung up the phone and went to grab some food out of the fridge. I was out, and had no money left. Then I got another call coming in.

"Alex?"

"Yes."

"This is Dick Wester from the press. I wonder if I can get some quotes from you?"

"Sure, any chance we can do it in person?"

"Errr, that's fine. Over coffee? The paper will pay?"

"Can we make it lunch?"

"Yeah, sure."

I arranged the place and time and once I'd hung up, I started walking that way out. I met Dick in the café and I ate a slap-up meal whilst he asked me how I felt; what it was like to be going to a home Olympics. I polished my meal off with a couple of beers and told him exactly what he wanted to hear: nighty per cent positive and happy, ten per cent scandal.

Dick, in his suit, headed back off to the office and I decided it was about time I went to pick up my car. I walked about two miles from the café to the car and, when I got there, it was covered in parking tickets. I opened the door and assumed the pushing position. Once I had her rolling, I tried the key. She struggled at first, but then I turned the key a second time and she jumped straight to it and started up.

53

I lived out the rest of the month in the flat, and at the end of the month I packed my car with everything that was mine and handed the keys back to the agent. The Olympics started in two weeks, and went on for a month, but I could move into the village whenever I needed to.

I called Coach to tell him that I was heading down to London. He drove over and gave me a jump-start on the car. Once she was running, I gave him my two free tickets to the games and he shook my hand.

"Good luck, Alex."

I smiled back at him, got into the car and drove down to London. It took just over five hours. When I arrived at the village, I parked up but left the car running. I got out and walked to the British registration desk. I handed them my passport at the check-in desk; they printed me off an ID card and took my car keys off me.

"Oh, the car won't start again if you turn it off. At least not easily."

"That's alright sir, I can have that looked at for you whilst you're here at the games."

"Oh no, don't pal, I've not got any money."

"That's not a problem, sir, we'll do it free of charge."

They gave me a slip for my car and they drove it to a huge car park for the duration of the games. I saw the guy look strangely as he saw a chair, drawers and my duvet in the back.

A very attractive, older lady escorted me round the village on my first night. She showed me the dining hall - where all the food was free. There was a communal bar, that didn't serve alcohol, but it had pool tables and dartboards. Coffee stands were outside most of the larger building, and any time of day you could grab a freshly made cup. She showed me the hospital, dentist and pharmacy: all free.

When we finally got to my room, she gave me a bag full of condoms and another bag full of Olympic pin badges. I dropped my bags into the room and went to the bar. I asked the guy behind the counter.

"Do you guys have anything alcoholic?"

"We don't have any alcohol, sir, this is a dry camp, but..." he looked at my pin badge, "I can get you a bottle of something for a pin?"

"A pin? That's all you want?"

"Yeah."

"Okay."

He went out back and came back in with a bottle of Southern Comfort. He gave it to me and I passed him the pin badge.

"You can't drink that in here though, alright pal?"

"Yeah, that's fine."

I took the bottle back to my room and sat on the bed listening to the radio whilst drinking the Southern Comfort.

54

The village started to get busy; my apartment was no longer just for me. I had a weightlifter in one room and a cyclist in the other. I was still able to get a few bottles of drink from the guy at the bar. I had to exchange other bits of Olympic kit for it, but he hadn't asked for too much really. And since the kit was free to me, I didn't mind so much.

I'd head out mid-morning and grab a coffee from one of the stalls outside the apartment buildings; food and drink in the village was free, and I was eating well off it. I had months of malnutrition to catch up on. I'd grab a coffee and then head for breakfast - so much to choose from: cooked foods from all over the world. The first week I ate cooked breakfasts, then, as the village started to get busier, I moved onto porridge.

Even as the games started, the village didn't seem full. I still had a room to myself and my barman was still covertly supplying me with booze. I trained most afternoons. In the evenings, I'd pick a sport and head into the Olympic Park to watch. The first time I went out, I was dressed in the Olympic kit. I didn't make that mistake again. Dressed in regular clothes, I could get in most places just by flashing my ID and offering a pin as my entrance fee.

I walked into the athletics on the 100m finals' evening. I got myself a beer with a flash of my ID, and I gained entrance to the stadium with a pin and a GB cap. The atmosphere was unreal - the noise that the crowd made. There wasn't a lick of air in the stadium, just other people's breath. I couldn't find a seat, so I perched on the steps up near the top, trying to stay out of everyone's way. A steward came to move me, I gave him a pin, and then about 20 minutes later another steward came up asking for a pin.

I saw Bolt do this thing on the track and take the win. The other guys following behind, tripping over themselves as they leaned for the line. Meanwhile, Bolt was just cruising round with his arms opened up towards the skies. I drained the beer and headed out before the masses tried to exit the stadium.

55

I arrived back in my room and there was a new bag thrown across the spare bed. I put on the radio and sat back on my bed. I reached under my pillow and pulled out a bottle, unscrewed it and had a quick nip. Then I quickly dropped it back under the pillow.

After a half hour, this huge guy walked in through the door.

"You Alex?"

"Yeah."

"Hi." He extended his hand to shake mine. "I'm Cid, gonna be rooming with you for the rest of the games."

I shook his hand and left him to unpack. I took another nip whilst he was sorting out his pack, then I went to the toilet and dropped a long overdue crap.

Once I was done, I came out and closed the door. I wanted to keep the smell in, but it had found a way through the cracks to escape. I took another hit of the whiskey and then jumped into bed and under the covers. I turned off my light and left Cid with just his side light on to unpack.

56

I woke up that night with the worst toothache. I took what painkillers I had in my bag, but it didn't help. I was tossing and turning for hours. I decided to drink some whiskey. I held it against the tooth that was causing me pain; trying to numb it up. I checked the clock: 3am. I drank and tossed about the bed some more: 5am. I finally dropped off and woke early with the pain setting in again.

I couldn't eat breakfast. I went to the dentist in the village. I sat in agony for nearly four hours waiting to be seen. I finally got in and jumped onto the bed.

"Hello, what's the problem here?"

"Toothache, Doc." I pointed the tooth out to him. "This one, and it's real bad. I couldn't sleep last night - it just came on."

"Okay, well let's have a look."

He tapped against it with his finger, then with the small mirror.

"Argh, fuck!" I jumped upwards off the bed.

"That's the tooth then?"

"Yeah, that's the fucking tooth."

"Okay, I'll give you these - you take them and come back in a couple of days."

I took the pills off him and left the clinic. I swallowed some straight down. I still couldn't eat food, but the drink helped take the pain away a little. I knocked back some more painkillers and a quarter bottle of whiskey. That night I still couldn't sleep, so I took a sleeping pill and washed it down with a nip of the whiskey. The pain was so bad that all I could do was grab the odd ten minutes as I tossed in bed. I took another sleeping pill and left the apartment block heading out for a late night walk around the village. About a half hour after I'd taken the pill, it smashed me down to the floor like a sledgehammer. I was out. I hit the deck and just lay in the centre of a grass feature.

I was woken the next morning by the sprinkler system. I still couldn't face food. I looked at my watch: 06.30. I walked to the dentist and sat outside until the doors opened at 9am. I was first in. I jumped onto the dentist table.

"I need this thing out or something Doc."

He bent over and went into my mouth. "Okay, I'll try a root canal, hopefully stop the pain for you. It will hurt though."

"Just do it, Doc, I can't keep things as they are."

57

My mouth was incredibly painful afterwards, and I hadn't slept properly for a good few days. I took some more painkillers and sat in my room with the radio on. Cid brought me a couple of bottles of water. I took a sleeping pill and just lay in bed all day groggy. I came to about midnight and took another sleeping pill that knocked me out until the next morning. I still couldn't face food in the morning, but I was hungry. I went to the food court and tried some soup; I managed to eat about half of it before I decided to head back to my room and lay down some more.

The next day, my mouth felt okay, still sore, but I could eat. I went into the dining hall and piled up my plate. I had chicken, burgers, potatoes, yams, pizza; I topped it all off with a bottle of coke and some yogurts for afters.

I walked out of the hall with a full belly; I stopped and grabbed a coffee on my way back to the apartment. I lay down and listened to the Olympics on the radio. I had a window open and I could hear the crowed cheer before the radio announcement came through. There seemed to be a four or five second delay on the broadcast. I lay there and pushed my finger into my mouth, feeling around my teeth, pushing and flicking each individual tooth checking for pain.

I heard the crowd roar for a new British record. The man on the radio was going crazy. In all that chaos, all I thought was that the man on the radio sounded like he was a small fella.

58

The day before the first round of the relay, I turned up at a relay practice. Spack, Jig, Slime and Terry were already there, along with Coach Carl.

"Nice of you to join us, Grindley."

"Nobody told me what time practice started."

"C'mon, Grindley. You see these guys often enough around the village. It's your job to find one of them and find out about practices."

"What? Isn't it your job to tell us about practices?"

"I'm not your fucking coach, Grindley."

"You're the Relay Coach."

"Shut the fuck up and get in the line."

He pointed to the changeover box. I walked into it with the other guys.

"Slime and Jig, run into Terry and Spack. Grindley, you just sit in the changeover box and simulate another country, be some interference or something."

They ran the first one in hard and fast.

"What the fuck are you gimps doing? You honestly think you'll be finishing like that at the end of a quarter mile? Slow it down," bellowed Coach Carl.

The next one was more on pace. I stood behind Spack and pressed my forearm into his back to hold space, he took the baton from Jig and pushed off my arm into Terry, he clipped his leg from behind and Terry went down.

"Stop, stop guys! Terry, you good?" asked Coach Carl.

"Yeah, Coach, just hit the knee a bit hard."

"Okay, well, we'll stop there then. I've seen what I need

to see."

"I've not changed a stick yet, Coach," I said.

"Grindley, come here." I walked over to him. "You guys go. I'll see you all tomorrow: 9am bus. I'll name the team then." The guys walked off and headed back into the village.

"Coach."

"Grindley. Shut the fuck up. You ever speak to me like you did today and you'll never run on a squad, okay? We have a good system here. I know the guys and they know me. You can't just turn up and mess with the group cohesion. Now I'll see you tomorrow. 9am bus."

59

I turned up at 08.50 for the bus; I stood and waited until 9.20 when the guys all turned up with Coach Carl.

"Hey where were you guys?"

"We went for a team breakfast before we head out," said Jig.

I got on the bus and it took us to the warm-up track. The Olympic stadium was a stone throw away and you could hear the crowd gathering and making their way into the ground.

I walked with the guys along a row of white tents, each

one displaying a different nation's flag. At the end of the 100m straight was a GB flag. I dumped my bag in there and headed out to jog round. I warmed up with the team.

A call went out on the PA system: "Heats of the Men's 4 x 400m relay, five minutes to call."

We all headed towards Coach Carl.

"Gather round, guys," he said. "Right. This is how it is: this is the team and I don't want to hear any shit. Just accept what I say and go and run. My first leg is Jig, he'll pass to Spack. I've spoken to Terry and he's got the knee strapped, but he'll be running third and, finally, Slime is gonna bring us home. Grindley, I just couldn't see how you'd fit the team so just sit this one out. Right guys go off and run."

I walked off and headed into the stadium. I watched the guys run; they finished first in the heat and qualified for the final. On my way out I passed Coach Carl again.

"Coach, how come I'm not in the squad?"

"It's like this, Grindley, you just haven't been working out with the team for long enough."

"But it's a relay? I just run 400m and pass the stick, surely I'm fast enough?"

"Well, yeah, you are. But you only came out to the camp earlier this year. You just have to serve your time on the bench at a few champs first. Now I don't want to hear anything about it, Grindley. Just accept it. The boys have a job to do tomorrow so just let things lie."

60

I was already at the warm-up track when Coach Carl and his boys turned up for the final of the 4 x 400m. I warmed up with the team as I did the day before. Half way through the warm up, Coach Carl shouted out to Terry.

"How's the knee?"

"Fucked Coach."

"It'll last buddy. You deserve this chance to run. I know how hard this has been. Suck it up and it'll be fine."

At the end of warm up Coach Carl called us all in again. "Guys, same team as yesterday. Everyone good? You all know what's happening?"

Everyone nodded their head and walked off to the stadium. I watched the team run on the big screen outside the venue. The boys came fourth, missing a medal by 0.11. Terry was laid out on the track holding his knee after the race - he hadn't run well. The commentators were suggesting he was nearly a second down on what was expected from him; a full two seconds slower than what I had been running all year.

I didn't hang around. I tried to blend with the crowd and

walk out into London. My kit gave me away; people were asking for pictures and wanting to talk. It was peculiar to me how these strangers would talk to you like you were their best friends. Parents would tell me how proud they felt, as their children gazed on wondering if they would ever gain their parents' recognition in the same way as this stranger had done.

61

I made it into the city. I took the tube to Liverpool Street Station and walked the streets looking for a bar. I saw a place that looked okay so I walked in and sat down.

"I'll have a beer, please."

The barman nodded and got me a bottle.

"You an athlete?"

"Yeah."

"How did ya do?"

"Didn't, was a team sport and I didn't get my chance."

"Sorry to hear that, mate, this one's on the house."

"Cheers, mate."

I took the beer and drained it quickly.

"Another, mate, please."

He placed the second down in front of me and an old guy a few seats down shouted out. "I got this one."

I picked up the beer and held it up to him to thank him and then drank it half way down quickly.

"You drinking away the blues?' asked the geezer.

"Maybe, if you think there needs to be a reason to drink."

"Better ways than this if you ask me."

"What's them then?"

"Girls and tits."

"If only it was that easy, eh, fella?"

He moved a few seats up to come next to me. "It can be, finish up and I'll take you to this joint around the corner, plenty of girls, nice girls. All just trying to find an easy life innit."

I drank up and followed him to this place. It looked nice, blue neon sign outside and a picture of a girl in a cocktail glass next to the sign 'slagheap'. There was a bouncer on the door with a list. The geezer pointed out my tracksuit and whispered into the bouncer's ear, and then we were in. I walked up to the bar and the barmaid leaned in close to me. She had a low cut top on and huge tits bouncing out towards me.

"What can I get you?" she whispered softly in my ear with a beautiful soft accent from the northeast. She pulled her lips close to mine as she finished and held a close eye contact. I could feel her breath touching my lips.

"Couple of beers please, love."

"Comin' right up, babe."

I paid for the beers and dropped one to the old fella. We sat at a table close to the bar. We were there about two minutes when a couple of plastic babes came over.

"Mind if we join you?"

"Please do," said the geezer.

"What do you ladies keep yourself busy with?" he asked.

"Whatever keeps us with a drink in hand."

"Or something else in hand," the other added; they turned, giggling.

The old fella signalled for a round of drinks to the table.

"What do you and your friend do?" asked the girl on the right of the geezer.

"I own a newsagents, and my mate. Can't you see? With the tracksuit? He is an Olympian."

The drinks came over and we all drained them quickly; then the fella ordered another load for the table.

We sat there a little while longer. The old guy and his chick took off after a few more rounds. After they had gone, the other girl leaned in close to me.

"You wanna get out of here babe?"

"Sure, but I gotta tell you, I don't actually know your name."

"That doesn't matter, sweetie, call me what you want, and for a hundred you can do what you want."

"I don't have a hundred babe."

"Seventy then, babe, you're hot so I don't mind taking a hit."

"Babe, I got nothing. I don't even have anywhere to live when I leave the Olympic village tomorrow."

"What? Nothing? You must have something. What you got?"

"Nothing, babe, I'm broke."

"Fuck this shit." She got up from the table and headed off to some other table with some old guys sat there.

The barmaid came over again with a bottle of beer. She put it down on the table then pulled up a seat.

"I had a bet with myself that you wouldn't walk out with a prossie."

"Yeah? What was that bet?"

"This beer."

"Thanks. You know I'm not from round here though?"

"I figured. I could hear your accent. I just felt like doing something nice for a nice guy, you know?"

"Yeah, I hear you. What's your name?"

"Emma Louise."

"Well hi, I'm Alex."

"Hi."

She chuckled and shook my hand.

"Enjoy your beer, Alex."

"I will thanks. Hey, what time do you finish tonight?"

"Oh not tonight, Alex, I don't want you to get the wrong idea about me."

I finished my beer alone; I kept glancing Emma's way and she'd see me looking and smile.

62

I packed my bag the next morning and went to the main security entrance. I gave my pass and my keys to a woman.

"Ah, Mr Grindley, your car is ready. It's been taken care of by our mechanical volunteers. Hope you had a fantastic Olympics, Mr Grindley."

"Thanks."

I took my car keys and walked out front. My car was sat waiting for me with my belongings inside. I put my bag on the passenger seat and jumped in the driver's side. I buckled up and took a look at the Olympic Village and then I set off through London, heading back up north.

I turned up at Coach's apartment. Parked up and sat there. I looked at his door. It was dark now, just gone 11pm. I decided not to bother him, so I slept in the car.

I was woken the next morning by a knocking on my window. I opened the window and looked up at Coach.

"Hi."

"Alex, I thought I was meeting you at the track today?"

"I need a day to sort myself out, Coach. I gotta find somewhere to live."

"Okay, Alex. You going to be okay?"

"Yeah, of course. I'll see you tomorrow."

I drove around for a couple of hours, round side streets trying to find something to let. Eventually, I saw a sign outside a hostel so I parked up and went to have a look.

I walked in and the building manager was sat in his room with the door open - it was directly to the right of the entrance.

"Hey, I don't know you. What can I do for you, pal?"

"I saw the sign out front. You have a room?"

"Yeah, pal, it's a hundred a month, a studio apartment, this is an old hostel that's been converted into studio flats. You wanna see the room?"

"No, it's fine. I'll take it."

"Sure thing, boss. I'll need the first month in advance."

"I can't get it to you now, but I'll give you my car keys to hang onto? Just till I get the money to you. I'll have it soon."

"What car you got?"

"Does it matter? Any car is worth at least a hundred."

"Yeah, okay. Just sign here. You're in number 4 on the first floor."

I signed the form and handed over my car keys in

exchange for my flat keys.

"Cheers mate."

The building manager took his leave and went back to his room. I unloaded my car and walked into my room. It was all right: had a bed and TV. I opened the fridge and found a couple of beers had been left in there along with half a sandwich. I opened the sandwich and smelt it, then immediately threw it out. I moved some stuff around the room and then opened a beer.

63

The next morning, I woke up and there was a bottle of warm beer next to my bed. It was barely drunk. I picked it up and put it to my lips. I was going to take a long pull when my phone went off. I pulled the bottle away from my lips and read the message from Coach: Hey are you actually gonna come and do some training today? I thought you were sorting your life out?

I threw the phone on the bed and left it there. I put the bottle to my lips and took a long hard pull. As I drank, I saw myself in the mirror. My six-pack abs had gone; there was even a gut starting to fold over my pants. On the floor, I saw my training shoes. I picked up the pair with my right hand while my left hand was still grasping the long, sleek neck of the beer.

I wanted to make a grand gesture to myself. I wanted to prove that I could do something worthwhile. I wanted to throw the beer. Throw it away. As I was sat there getting ready to throw this bottle, my left hand had unconsciously moved the bottle to my lips a few more times. It was about half way down and I looked at the bottle. I took another pull. A quarter left. One final long pull as I drained the beer.

I threw it over my shoulder. I moved to put on my training shoes but heard the thud of the bottle impacting behind me, so I turned to look. My damn left hand had been like a stranger to me; it had thrown the bottle with no regard for the contents of my studio apartment and had taken out my TV.

"Fuck!"

I picked up my phone, scrolled to my messages and replied to Coach: 'Got some personal stuff I need to take care of today. Will be in tomorrow'.

I threw the training shoes back onto the floor and moved towards the cupboard under the sink. I grabbed a bottle of whiskey, poured a half pint of it and mixed it with water. I sat down on my bed as if to watch TV, but then I saw again that it was smashed.

I moved to an old laptop that I'd bought off a bum for a couple of quid. I booted it up and opened a Word document. I kept sipping at the whiskey, and when it got low I'd top it up. I sat and wrote. I wrote shit. I wrote stories. I documented my life. I wrote dirty stories. I wrote naughty poems. I wrote a message to

Emma Louise. I kept drinking heavily throughout. I had to squint to see the words in front of me. Then I ran out of booze, so walked down to a pub. I sat out in the beer garden drinking, until eventually I got asked to leave at closing time. I walked home with a bottle of beer. By the time I got home, it was half empty. I left it on my bedside table; took my clothes off and got under the covers. I decided to have a wank, but after flicking at my cock for a while, nothing was happening. So I closed my eyes and slept. Waking the next morning next to a half bottle of beer.

ABOUT THE AUTHOR

Richard Buck is a British born author. He grew up in rural Yorkshire. Richard moved to Leeds in 2006, to study for his undergraduate degree and pursue his athletic ambitions.

Richard became a Freeman of York in 2013.

6742653R00109

Printed in Great Britain
by Amazon.co.uk, Ltd.,
Marston Gate.